FOR PRINCESS

IT TAKES MORE THAN GOOD GRADES TO GRADUATE FROM CENTRAL ACADEMY . . .

Discover the chilling adventures that shadow the halls and stalk the students of
TERROR ACADEMY!

LIGHTS OUT

Mandy Roberts digs up the suspicious past of the new assistant principal. The man her widowed mother plans to marry . . .

STALKER

A tough punk comes back to Central with one requirement to complete: vengeance . . .

SIXTEEN CANDLES

Kelly Langdon discovers there's more to being popular than she thought—like staying alive . . .

SPRING BREAK

It's the vacation from hell. And it's up to Laura Hollister to save her family. And herself . . .

THE NEW KID

There's something about the new transfer student. He's got a deadly secret . . .

continued . . .

STUDENT BODY

No one's safe at Central—
when a killer roams the halls . . .

NIGHT SCHOOL

The most handsome teacher in school . . .
is a vampire!

SCIENCE PROJECT

There's a new formula for terror:
E = mc scared . . .

THE PROM

It's a party that could raise the dead . . .

THE IN CROWD

A group of misfits learn a deadly lesson:
if you don't fit in, you may be out—
for good!

SUMMER SCHOOL

Making up is hard to do — when terror is
waiting at summer school . . .

TERROR ACADEMY

BREAKING UP

NICHOLAS PINE

MAMMOTH

First published in the United States of America 1994
by Berkley Books, an imprint of the Berkley Publishing Group
First published in Great Britain 1995
by Mammoth, an imprint of Reed Consumer Books Ltd
Michelin House, 81 Fulham Road, London SW3 6RB
and Auckland, Melbourne, Singapore and Toronto.

Copyright © 1994 by C. A. Stokes

ISBN 0 7497 2311 4

A CIP catalogue record of this title
is available from the British Library

Printed in Great Britain by
BPC Paperbacks Ltd
A member of
The British Printing Company Ltd

BREAKING UP

ONE

Robin Anderson shut her locker door and turned to walk down the hall to her English class. In the crowded corridor Robin stood out boldly, a statuesque blond girl who just happened to be going steady with the cocaptain of the Central Academy hockey team. As Robin glided between the other groups of students, most of the boys stole sidelong looks at the gorgeous-enough-to-be-a-model girl who belonged to Skip Chesterton. Of course, if any of them tried to make a move on Robin, Skip would pound them into little pieces, a fact that used to thrill her.

Robin nodded to one of her classmates, Candy Reed, who played on the girls' varsity field hockey team with Robin. Field hockey season had been over for a couple of months.

It was January, the beginning of a new semester. Time for Skip to shine on the ice.

Skip had made All-State as a center on the hockey squad. He was the star, something that had drawn Robin to him as a junior. Now she wasn't quite sure how she felt about Skip's fame. Not that she was jealous or anything. After all, Robin had been the captain of the girls' soccer team that had gone to the state finals last spring to beat Dover for the championship. Soccer was Robin's best sport and she liked it a lot more than field hockey.

Candy fell in beside Robin, trying to match the blond girl's healthy stride. "Hey. What's up?"

Robin shrugged and pushed a hand through her thick hair. "Just getting used to the old schedule again," she replied blankly.

"Are you going to the game tonight?" Candy asked.

Robin gave a sigh. "I guess."

Candy grimaced. "You guess?"

"I'll be there," Robin insisted testily. "Okay?"

"Well, Skip is starting," Candy replied, shaking her short-cropped auburn hair.

Candy had a major crush on Skip and Robin knew it. Candy wasn't as gorgeous as Robin, but she was still attractive. Blue eyes, dimpled chin, a freckled complexion that made her look wholesome. At one time, Robin had been worried about Candy's attraction to Skip. But now she wasn't sure it bothered her. Something had changed over Christmas break.

"Let's sit behind the bench so we can be close to Skip," Candy said. "If we—"

Robin glared at her. "Hey, why don't you just sit *on* the bench, Candy!"

Candy's face turned bright red. "But I—"

"Better yet—sit on Skip! I'm sure you'd love that."

Robin stormed away. She had never unloaded like that on Candy before. And she really wasn't angry at Candy for having a crush on Skip.

So why was she so quick to explode?

Rounding the corner, Robin stopped for a second, leaning back against the wall, closing her eyes. What was wrong with her? Why had she come back from Christmas vacation so sensitive and temperamental? After all, Skip had given her that ring, the one he called a pre-engagement symbol. Her parents had been so happy.

I'm a senior, she thought. *Going with the greatest guy in school, a guy who loves me. And I should love him. But do I?*

The ring had done it. Robin had been forced to look at the relationship with a serious eye. It wasn't like she didn't care about Skip. What was it?

A little voice in the back of her head offered one simple word: *BOREDOM!*

Robin shook her head, trying to clear the cobwebs. Her hair flew for a moment in several directions. She had to brush the long tresses from her face.

"Whoa, do that again, you hot babe. Owww!"

Robin gazed across the corridor in the direction of the male voice. Her blue eyes focused on one of the longhairs from Pitney Docks. He actually looked sort of cute in the leather jacket but Robin couldn't let him get away with this harassment.

"How 'bout me and you tonight?" the longhair said.

Wow, was he ever cute! A slender face, cool hazel eyes. But Robin wouldn't tolerate his attitude.

"Sorry," she said, grimacing. "I don't date outside my species, chimp-boy."

Someone stepped next to the longhair, another boy who wore a black overcoat and combat boots. "Hey, is he botherin' you, Miss Anderson? Huh?"

Robin immediately recognized the interloper. He was Danny Kovack from her English class. Danny was cool, attractive and forceful, but he had a reputation for being a delinquent.

Robin had caught herself studying him more than once in class. Everyone knew Danny rode a Harley, even in the winter, and he went steady with a girl who had already graduated.

The long-haired boy started to retreat. "Hey, Dan, I wasn't botherin' her—"

Danny, who was bigger than the other boy, grabbed him and put him in a headlock. "Now don't you bother this girl. Okay? She's something special!"

"Awright, Danny! Awright!"

He let go of the boy's head. "Now, say you're sorry."

"I'm sorry!"

The long-haired boy ran off down the hall.

Danny glanced back at her with his dark brown eyes. "A thousand pardons, mademoiselle!"

Robin found herself smiling at him. "Thanks, Danny."

"Did you do your English homework?" Danny asked.

Robin nodded. "Yes."

Danny made a face and shrugged. "I blew it off completely. What a jerk, huh?"

Robin wasn't sure how to reply. She couldn't take her eyes off Danny. He wasn't really cuter than Skip. In fact, Skip had it all over Danny. Except that Danny was rugged-looking and his personality was so different.

If he dressed better, he might even give Skip a run for his money.

"Are you okay, countess?" Danny asked.

Robin was about to reply when a hand fell on her shoulder.

"I was looking for you," Skip said, gazing into her eyes. "Is everything all right?"

Robin nodded absently, blushing as if she had been caught doing something wrong. "Oh, Skip . . ."

Skip turned to regard Danny Kovack, who was still smiling. Robin studied Skip's handsome face. He had black hair and green eyes, a combination that had slayed Robin when she was a junior.

But now I'm a senior, she thought.

"Kovack, what are you doing to my girl?" Skip asked.

Danny shrugged. "Nothing. Some geek was hitting on her and I sent him skating."

Skip glanced back at her. "He helped you?"

Robin nodded. "He's in my English class."

Skip's half scowl did not go away. "I'm not sure I want him—" He turned to glower at Danny, but the boy was gone.

Robin felt badly. "Skip!"

"That guy is a hound," Skip insisted. "He's a biker. You can't trust guys like that."

"He's not so bad," Robin replied. "He's kind of nice."

"Well, you just stay away from him." Skip

grabbed her hand. "This ring means that you belong to me, Robin."

Well, maybe I should give it back, she thought.

What would the student body say about the most popular couple at Central breaking up?

Skip smiled warmly, a once charming trait that was no longer that appealing. "Where are you gonna sit at the game tonight?"

Robin shrugged. "I don't know."

He frowned again. "What's wrong with you?"

"Skip . . ."

She didn't want to hurt him. He had been so sweet. Robin didn't blame him for being impatient.

"I'm going to sit behind the bench," she told him. "Candy and some of the other girls will be there too."

It was the easiest way to get rid of him.

Skip smiled again. "Great. You got a kiss for me?"

Their lips brushed lightly. Robin remembered deeper kisses, passionate embraces. But it all seemed so cold now. Had she simply lost it? Was that how the magic vanished in relationships?

Skip winked at her and headed in the direction of his sociology class. Robin moved again in the corridor, aware that the bell was going to ring at any moment. As she crossed through the doorway of her English class, the tardy signal pealed down the hall.

Easing into her desk, Robin lifted her eyes to see Mrs. Traxler glaring at her. She wasn't really late. But Mrs. Traxler was wound so tightly that she'd give a student a hard time for a close call.

"Glad you could make it, Miss Anderson."

Robin smiled weakly, thinking, *Bite it, you old geek.*

Mrs. Traxler fixed her eyes on Robin and started on some lecture about punctuality.

Robin looked away, gazing out the window. As Mrs. Traxler droned on, Robin felt something on her face. It was almost like a hot spot was forming on her skin.

Her eyes wandered back into the room, focusing on the face of Danny Kovack, who was grinning. He had just sent a note in Robin's direction. It was coming across the desks to her, a dispatch between rows.

Robin felt her heart pounding. Why would Danny send her a note? Moreover, why would she want to read it?

But she *did* want to read it!

Maybe he was inviting her to take a ride on his motorcycle.

She glanced quickly at Mrs. Traxler, who had turned toward the chalkboard. The note landed on her desk. Robin opened it quickly.

"Sorry about that punk bothering you,"

Danny had written. "If he keeps bugging you, let me know and I'll dust him for you. Your pal, Danny."

She looked at him again, her body tingling with a strange sensation. Why did he quicken her pulse? Why did she want to wrap her arms around him and ride screaming on the Harley through the streets of Port City? Good girls weren't supposed to want guys like Danny Kovack.

"Miss Anderson, excuse me? Miss Anderson?"

Robin gazed back at Mrs. Traxler, who was gawking at her. "Uh, yes?" Robin offered weakly.

Mrs. Traxler, a stout, gray-haired matron, looked down her long nose, staring through thick glasses. "Is there something you'd like to share with us, Miss Anderson?"

Robin, who hated being in trouble, shook her head. "No, I—"

Danny Kovack stood up quickly. "Uh, Ms. Trax, I was just asking Robin if she could help me with my homework. I've been having some trouble in your class."

Mrs. Traxler smiled, though it wasn't a sunny proposition. "I see. Well, you could certainly use a tutor, Mrs. Kovack. Would you like to volunteer?" she asked Robin.

Robin sat up straight. "Sure, why not?"

There was a gasp from almost everyone in the room.

Was Robin, one of the most popular girls at Central, really volunteering to help a ne'er-do-well? Robin came from Prescott Estates, the best section of Port City. Danny lived over by the waterfront in Pitney Docks. She swam at the country club, he rode a Harley that he had rebuilt in shop class. They weren't even supposed to talk to each other, much less study together.

Mrs. Traxler grinned sadistically, thinking she had embarrassed Robin. "Very well, then it's settled. You'll tutor Danny, Robin."

She lifted her pretty chin, glaring right back at the instructor. "Fine!"

Danny shook his head. "Wow."

Robin didn't care what anyone thought.

She was going to tutor Danny in English.

Robin *wanted* to tutor him. She just didn't know *why*!

Some of the other girls were whispering together.

Robin heard, "What will Skip say?"

What *would* Skip say? Robin thought.

She didn't care. Whether Skip liked it or not, Robin was going to spend time with Danny Kovack!

TWO

Robin's last class of the day was Physical Education. All members of varsity sports teams, male and female, were scheduled for final period Phys. Ed. so they could take advantage of an extra hour of practice. Since field hockey was a memory and soccer didn't start for three months, Robin and the rest of the class were allowed what the coach called "free gym," a time to lift weights, run and do calesthenics.

Robin went through the motions on the weight machine, doing some bench presses, but eventually she found a quiet corner to sit and think. She closed her eyes, repeating the fantasy of riding on the motorcycle with Danny Kovack. Why was she drawn to him? Danny had a reputation for being a rebel, a troublemaker.

11

At least he wasn't boring, Robin thought. He had some fire inside him. Skip and his group of jocks could get a little wild sometimes, but it was all too calculated, too tame. Danny had a mysterious air about him, an aura of danger. Something could happen at any place, anytime with Danny around.

Robin saw herself on the backseat of the Harley, her arms wrapped around Danny's waist, her face snuggled into his jacket. She could almost smell the exhaust and the leather. Where would they go on the Harley? To Lightning Point! Would he kiss her, igniting the flames that needed so desperately to kindle inside her?

Who was she kidding? Danny was from Pitney Docks, the son of a fry cook. Robin lived in Prescott Estates, the daughter of a surgeon at the community hospital. Skip was more her type. Skip also lived in Prescott Estates, the son of a wealthy shipbuilder from the shipyard. Skip's father owned the stretch of waterfront where Danny lived.

What would Robin's parents say if she brought home a guy like Danny? Yet, they had always allowed her to pick her own boyfriend—as long as he was a guy like Skip. She heard herself saying, "Hi, Mom and Dad, this is Danny. He's not as bad as you think. I mean, he never killed anyone."

"Hi, Robin, what are you doing back here by yourself?"

Robin opened her eyes to see Candy standing there. "Hi, Candy. Sorry I was so rude to you before."

Candy smiled triumphantly. "Yes, you were. But that's okay. Are you going to the hockey game tonight?"

Robin's brow fretted. "You know I am."

Why was Candy smirking like that?

Candy laughed a little. "Oh, I wasn't sure if you'd want to go after what I heard."

Robin's eyes narrowed. "Candy, what are you talking about?"

"Oh, nothing, just that you and Danny Kovack are an item now. It's all over the school."

Robin shook her head. "Get real."

"I heard you volunteered to tutor him in English," Candy went on. "He passed you a note too."

Robin glared at Candy. "If you don't shut up, Candy, I'm going to be rude to you again."

Candy put on an act that smacked of fake sincerity. "Oh, I understand what happened, Robin. I heard Mrs. Traxler pushed you into it. I just hope Skip understands."

Robin came off the bench where she had been sitting, brushing past Candy. "Get over it, Candy."

"What will Skip say?"

Robin wheeled around to confront Candy. "You want to know something? I don't care what Skip thinks!"

Candy said, "Really?"

"Just leave me alone," Robin told her. "And mind your own business, Candy."

"Well, Robin, I just thought as a friend—"

Robin chortled disgustedly. "Some friend. You've been after Skip ever since I started going out with him."

Candy's face showed anger for a moment. "That's not true!"

Robin returned the smirking expression. "Yeah? Well, the way you're acting, I can see that the truth hurts!"

"Robin—"

But it was too late. Robin stomped away to shower and change into her jeans, sweater and running shoes. She knew Candy was going to stir up trouble. But somehow, it didn't matter.

When her hair was dry, Robin went into the gym and sat in the bleachers for the rest of the period. The coach asked her what was wrong and Robin replied that she wasn't feeling well. Her excuse seemed to be good enough for the coach to leave her alone. Robin leaned back on the bleachers and returned to her daydreams.

Lately, Robin had been entertaining thoughts of wild parties, dancing all night, fast cars and dangerous boys. The Christmas vacation with Skip had been so dull. They had attended the annual dance at the country club, a few Christmas parties and dinners at the houses of their families.

A couple of times during the holiday break, Skip had tried to draw Robin into some heavy kissing sessions, but Robin had acted reluctant every time. What had happened between them to make her grow cold? Everything was the same as it had been when they were juniors.

"Everything is the same," Robin whispered to herself.

The same! That was the problem. Nothing ever changed between her and Skip.

Robin sighed, thinking about Danny Kovack again. He was cute in his own way. His haircut was a little spiky and he didn't dress very well. But he had nice eyes and a rugged look that attracted older girls to him.

Even if Robin could get a date with him, would she be able to handle a guy like Danny?

Maybe she should just play it safe with boring Skip, a guy who most girls would kill to go out with.

Robin's eyes wandered over the basketball court where the boys team was practicing at one end and the girls at the other. Candy had come into the gym to sit with a few of the sophomores and juniors from the girls jayvee basketball squad. She was laughing and whispering and pointing in Robin's direction. The other girls were laughing with her.

Robin rolled her eyes. "Real mature, Candy."

She tried to ignore them, but it was difficult. Nobody liked to be the object of gossip and ridicule. Of course, it was all part of Candy's scheme to get Skip away from her. Maybe it was time to just let Candy have him.

The bell rang, freeing her from the torture.

Robin hurried out of the gym, crossing the plaza toward the senior classroom building.

The sky had darkened over Port City, threatening snow for the quaint, seaside, New England village. A few flurries had already begun to flutter from the sky. Robin had left her overcoat in her locker. She'd need the heavier garment now that the wind was whipping along the Tide Gate River.

She entered the senior building and started for her locker. The halls were crowded, bustling with end-of-the-day activity. It was also a Friday, which meant that the weekend lay ahead, complete with the big hockey game at Municipal Arena. There was no ice facility at Central, so all of the games had to be played at the town rink. Robin certainly wasn't looking forward to watching another game with Skip as the main attraction.

Is it over? she wondered.

Or is this just a rough spot that will pass?

It's more than a rough spot.

When Robin reached her locker, her hand touched the combination dial of the lock. She saw the ring on her finger, the pre-engagement promise from Skip. It didn't mean anything to her. She wasn't going to be stuck for life with Skip. She had her whole life ahead of her, so there was no reason to get tied down now.

"Hey, foxy!"

Robin flinched. The voice was right behind her. Someone flopped on the wall of lockers, leaning back to smile at her.

Robin suddenly found herself smiling. "Oh, Danny, hi. How are you?"

Danny crossed his arms and shrugged. "Not too bad. Hey, sorry about all that garbage in English class."

Robin shrugged, wishing that her pounding heart would stop trying to make a hasty exit up into her throat. "That's okay. Mrs. Traxler is a butthead."

Danny sighed. "Man, I don't know how I'm gonna make it in that class. I mean, I try to study, but I hate that old witch so much, it makes me want to stop trying."

"I understand," Robin replied. "It's hard to

do well in a class where you hate the teacher."

Danny shook his head. "Everybody thinks I'm a screwup, Robin. But I'm getting B's in all my other classes. I'm gonna graduate and I've got money saved to go to Port City Community College. I know a rich kid like you is heading for an Ivy League school—"

Robin frowned. "What do you mean by a 'rich kid like me'?"

Danny's mouth tightened. "I—uh—you live in Prescott Estates and your father is a doctor."

"I don't think it's fair for you to judge me, Danny. You don't like to be judged, do you?"

"No, I guess not."

She pulled open her locker and took out her coat. "Good. I hope we understand each other."

"Uh, sure, let me help you with that."

Robin tingled all over as Danny assisted her with the overcoat. He seemed so different from his reputation. Maybe he was really a nice guy who had gotten a bum rap because he was from the wrong side of town. Maybe those rumors about partying, drinking and drug use were just lies.

"There you go," Danny said, stepping back.

Robin smiled again. "Thank you."

He blushed. Actually blushed! Did he like her? Had he been watching *her* in English class?

"Uh, I just wanted to say," Danny started. "Well, I—"

He looked directly into her eyes. His face slacked a little. He seemed to lose concentration.

Robin gazed back at him, thinking that with a new haircut and a fresh set of clothes, Danny would actually be quite handsome. "Yes, Danny?"

"Wow, you sure look beautiful. I—I mean . . . Sorry. Hey!" He snapped back to reality, assuming a cocky posture. "Look, I know the Trax pushed you to the wall on this tutoring deal. But I'm not gonna hold you to it."

Robin grimaced. "What?"

"You don't have to tutor me," Danny replied. "I know she forced you into it. I don't want to embarrass you."

Robin sighed. "Look, cheese-head, I want to tutor you, okay?"

His dark eyes grew wide. "Really?"

"Really. Now, why don't you call me at home and we can—uh, oh—it's Skip!"

She caught sight of the red and white letter sweater. Skip swaggered down the hall with a gang of his hockey friends. He hadn't seen Robin and Danny standing together.

Robin pushed Danny away. "Go."

"Hey, I'm not afraid of—"

"Just go," Robin insisted.

"But you're gonna tutor me!"

Robin smiled. "Do you like hockey?"

"I hate it."

"So do I," Robin replied, "but come to the arena tonight!"

"Sure, okay—"

"Go!"

Danny scuttered off down the hall.

Robin turned toward Skip. He was charging toward her now. His face had grown red and angry. Skip had seen her with Danny. And he wasn't too happy about it.

THREE

Skip's approach was like a disturbing dream to Robin. She saw his angry face, heard his barking voice. But the whole thing did not register with Robin. Suddenly she felt an emotional detachment that allowed her to look into Skip's eyes with a blank expression on her pretty face.

"I told you," Skip went on, "I don't want you hanging around with that guy!"

Robin just sighed and nodded, thinking what a jerk Skip was for berating her. After all, she was a free person. She could talk to anyone she chose. She certainly didn't need Skip's permission to lead her own life.

"Danny is trouble!" Skip railed. "Do you want to hang out with that sort of person?"

Robin shrugged, half listening. "I don't

21

know, Skip. I mean, I *have* to tutor him. Mrs. Traxler said so."

"I don't care what Mrs. Traxler said, you have to stay away from him," Skip said.

"I'm not a baby," Robin replied calmly. "And you're not my father, Skip."

Skip put his hands on his hips. "Oh? What would your father say if he knew you were hanging out with a guy like that? Robin, you better listen to me or—"

His voice seemed to fade. Robin glanced to her left to see Candy lurking in the hallway, smiling. Candy was ready to help Skip pick up the pieces. Robin wondered what Skip would do if she really broke it off.

Boredom!

His voice tuned in again. "—could be in trouble, Robin. Do you hear me?"

Robin smiled. "Uh-huh."

Skip took a deep breath and said, "Geez, I don't know what I'm going to do with you."

She grimaced. "Don't worry about it."

"But I do worry," Skip replied. "Sometimes you seem so distant lately, like you're in another world."

Yeah, a world that's not boring!

Skip took her hand again. "Doesn't this ring mean anything to you, Robin?"

She hesitated. "Skip, maybe—maybe we should talk about this. I mean—"

He waved her off. "No way. You're mine,

Robin. You'd better get that through your head right now." He grinned as if his caveman boasting was impressive.

BOR-ING!

Robin sighed. "Skip."

He put his hands on her shoulders. "Hey, who's my girl?"

"Skip, please—"

He drew her close, embracing her. "We're gonna be together forever, babe. You got that?"

Robin could see Candy at the other end of the hall. Candy's expression had changed into a grim mask. Candy turned and hurried away, disappointed that Skip and Robin seemed to be making up after all.

Skip drew back finally. "Hey, got a kiss for your lover man?"

Robin shrugged, ignoring him.

He lowered his lips.

Robin turned her head so he could only brush her cheek.

Skip gave her a quizzical expression. "I guess I'll never figure you out."

You've got that right!

"See you at the game?" Skip asked.

She remembered that Danny had promised to come to the hockey game at Municipal Arena. "Uh, yeah, I'll be there."

"I knew I could count on my girl," Skip replied.

Skip's friends called to him, saying that they had better hurry or they would be late for the team meeting.

"I gotta go," Skip told her. "You love me?"

Robin nodded, figuring it was the easiest way to get rid of him. "Sure."

Skip gave her that stupid smile that had once thrilled her to the marrow. Now he seemed like a foolish jock. Was this how it felt to lose feelings for someone? Skip had been her only serious boyfriend, but now she couldn't stand the sight of him.

Robin retrieved her books from her locker and started down the corridor. She had driven her Ford Escort to school and it was parked in the special lot set aside for seniors. Her parents had purchased the powder-blue Escort on Robin's sixteenth birthday. As she walked toward the lot, she heard the motorcycle screeching away from the school. For a moment she caught a glimpse of Danny Kovack on his Harley.

How could he ride his motorcycle on such a cold day?

He's tough, Robin thought.

Maybe too tough.

But she was drawn to him. Maybe spending time with Danny would destroy her fascination. Maybe it would make her appreciate Skip again.

Robin drove home through the narrow

streets of Port City. The town looked barren
after the end of the Christmas holidays. A
snow had fallen recently, but most of it was
now dirty and grainy. It would take another
snowstorm to recover Port City with a blan-
ket of white. A few flurries were dropping
from the sky, but Robin wasn't sure it would
turn into real snow.

On Middle Road, she passed Old Cemetery
and then Tremont Mall. The entrance of
Prescott Estates was marked by two stone
walls on either side of the street. Robin
entered the neighborhood that was a mixture
of colonial, Victorian and modern houses.
Sometimes Robin hated being the daughter
of a well-to-do surgeon. There was so much
expected of her as one of the popular kids.

The Escort slid into the driveway of the
two-story Victorian home that boasted a view
of the Tide Gate River and the New Market
Bridge. Her parents weren't home yet, so
when Robin entered the house, it was dark
and empty. She flopped down on the sofa in
the living room and sat in the shadows,
watching as the snowfall became heavier
outside.

"What am I going to do?" she asked herself.

The phone rang, startling her.

When Robin answered, there was silence
from the other end of the line.

"Who is this?" she demanded.

No reply.

"This isn't funny! You'd better tell me—"

Click!

She hung up. *Someone playing games,* she thought.

Robin had no idea that the games were just beginning.

When Danny braked the Harley in front of his father's diner, the bike slid to a halt on the icy street. The heavy snow made it difficult to drive the motorcycle in the winter. But Danny persisted with his biker image, mainly because he thought it made him look dangerous. Not that he *was* dangerous. Danny simply would not fall into the character molds accepted by the ruling cliques at Central Academy. He couldn't be a jock, a nerd or a wanna-be, so he chose to be a tough guy, which wasn't hard since most of the kids at Central were real wimps anyway.

Danny climbed off the Harley and spun toward the diner's greasy front window. His father, a potbellied man in his late fifties, had just hung the CLOSED sign on the glass. Danny went in to the diner, immediately noticing that his father's bottle of whiskey was already sitting on the counter. His old man had closed early so he could get a jump on his drinking.

"Closing already, Pop?" Danny asked.

Laslo Kovack grunted and scratched his grizzled face. "The snow's killin' business today."

Yeah, and I'll bet you're gonna kill that bottle.

Danny poured himself a cup of coffee and watched as his father downed a shot of whiskey. "Want me to clean up, Pop?"

"Nah, I'll do it."

Danny usually worked in the diner after school, cooking and waiting on tables. The clientele wasn't exactly the cream of Port City society, but he had managed to sock away his tip money. His father also paid him minimum wage and it was cash in hand with no taxes taken out.

Danny took a sip of the lukewarm coffee. "Sure there's nothing you want me to do?"

Mr. Kovack shook his head. "Nah. You go on, take the day off. I plan to."

Danny put down the cup and reached behind the counter, grabbing the cover for his Harley. Returning to the street, he covered the bike and tied off the seams around the spokes of the tires. Back inside the diner, Danny grabbed his coffee, refilled the cup and then climbed a set of stairs to the apartment above the diner.

The apartment was a hole, even though Danny had tried to fix up his own room. He would leave the waterfront one day. He would get an education, something he had promised his mother when she was on her deathbed, succumbing to the cancer that devastated her frail body. Things hadn't been so bad before his mother died. But after her death, his father had started drinking and the diner began to go downhill. Danny couldn't hate his father, who was never a mean drunk. Laslo Kovack used the whiskey to dull his pain and grief. Danny had simply learned to live with the same emotions.

Danny finished the coffee and fell on his bed, gazing out the window at the river. The snow was now steady, dropping huge, wet flakes on Port City. Soon, the snowplows would be running up and down the streets, pushing the white stuff into high embankments.

Danny sighed and picked up the phone next to his bed. He punched the number and waited for the girl to answer. She sounded glad to hear him. Her name was Doreen and she worked in a restaurant at the mall. Danny had met her the previous summer, when Doreen had briefly worked the breakfast shift at the diner.

"Are we goin' out tonight?" she asked.

"Sure. How do you feel about the hockey game?"

Doreen made a disappointed sound. "The hockey game?"

"Yeah, Central Academy is playing."

Doreen sighed. "I thought you didn't like any of those geeks at your school."

"I figured I'd take a chance," Danny replied. "Hey, we don't have to go. Want to hit a movie?"

"I thought we'd get a video and relax at my place," Doreen replied. "Is that okay?"

"Sure, babe. Maybe we could get something to eat after—"

"Sounds good, Danny-boy. Hey, my boss is lookin'. I gotta go. See ya."

Danny hung up the phone and looked out the window again. He had promised Robin that he would meet her at the game. Would she be disappointed? Probably not.

After he had left her in the hall, Danny had stood nearby, watching Skip and Robin around a corner. He had seen them embracing, kissing. Danny didn't have a chance with a girl like Robin, even though he had been hoping.

Robin was beautiful, classy, elegant. Danny had always wanted to be with a girl like Robin, but he had a *reputation*. Sure, he had done some things in his past, had made a few mistakes, but he'd cleaned up his act. A girl like Robin, though, would never go for him.

It would only cause trouble if he tried to date her.

Danny didn't like trouble anymore.

Sometimes, however, trouble seemed to like *him*.

FOUR

Danny smiled and gazed into Robin's eyes. His hands were holding her shoulders, caressing her, proving his strength and his tenderness in the same moment. Robin felt weak, helpless. Skip had never made her feel this way, not even in the beginning when things were good between them.

"I love you, Danny," Robin whispered.

He tensed, his biceps straining the sleeves of his T-shirt. "No girl ever made me feel this way, Robin."

"I know. I know, Danny."

Suddenly he broke away, fleeing from their embrace. "It won't work, Robin. You're too popular. I'm all wrong for you. I'll just bring you down."

She put her hand on his shoulder, gently

31

turning him toward her. "Let me be the judge of that, Danny."

He smiled bashfully. She had known he would have a shy side. All that posing and blustering couldn't fool Robin. She knew what Danny had in his heart.

"You think we could make it?" Danny asked. "I need to hear you say it."

She nodded, smiling back. "I think we can make it, Danny."

"What about your parents?"

"Let me worry about them," Robin replied.

A bleating noise seemed to rise from nowhere.

Robin frowned and looked away. "What's that?"

"Hey, you gotta kiss for me?"

Her jaw dropped. Robin wheeled back, gazing into Skip's expectant face. How had Skip gotten here?

The ringing noise persisted in her head.

"Skip—"

He grabbed her roughly. "You're mine. Forever. You won't have to think one thought. You'll just do whatever I tell you. Don't worry about being your own person, Robin. I'll run your whole life."

Sweat broke on her forehead. "No way!"

He took her hand. "This ring—"

Robin pulled back. "Screw the ring, I'm

with Danny. He's the one I care about, not you."

"Don't be silly," Skip replied. *"You know what day this is?"*

Robin trembled. "What?" she asked, fearing the answer.

"Our wedding day!" Skip howled. "We're getting hitched!"

He pulled her toward him.

The ringing would not stop.

Suddenly Robin was wearing a white gown and a veil. Skip had on a tuxedo. She heard the wedding march swelling in the air.

"No!"

The ringing seemed louder.

"I won't marry him!"

A deep voice boomed alongside the persistent bleating. "Do you, Skip, take Robin to be your lawfully wedded wife?"

"I do!"

Where was that ringing coming from?

"Do you, Robin—"

"No! Noooo!"

Robin sat up. A lone bead of perspiration streaked down her face. She had fallen asleep, and now the phone was ringing next to her bed.

"Hello?"

"Uh, Robin?"

She didn't recognize the voice at first. "Who is this?"

A hesitation on the other end of the line made Robin remember the hang-up call that afternoon.

"Uh, Robin, this is Paige—"

"Paige!"

"Uh, if you're busy, Robin, I can—"

"No, I was just taking a nap. Let me clear my head."

Paige had been Robin's best friend until Robin started going steady with Skip. Skip's possessiveness kept her away from everyone, including all of her old friends. Robin had known Paige since second grade. Yet she had let Skip push Paige out of her life.

Paige was a nice girl, a cute brunette with green eyes and an upturned nose. They had played together on the field hockey team. They had done a lot of things together before Skip came along. Where did he get off trying to run Robin's life?

"Robin?"

"Sorry, Paige. Hi. I'm so glad you called. What's up?"

Paige sighed. "Listen, I hope you don't think I'm a dink for asking this, but I heard you had a fight with Skip today."

Robin leaned back on her bed, sighing. "Yeah?"

"Look, if I'm butting in—I mean, it's all over school that something happened between you and Danny Kovack."

"I—I don't know, Paige. I'm so confused."

Robin suddenly realized how much she had missed Paige, how much she needed to talk to her.

"Robin, I was wondering—"

"I'm going to the hockey game tonight, Paige. Do you want to go with me?"

"Sure, but we're gonna have to hurry. It's almost seven o'clock and the game starts at seven-thirty."

Robin sat up. "I'll hurry. You want me to drive?"

"All right. Robin?"

"What?"

"Is everything all right?" Paige asked.

Robin exhaled. "No."

"What's wrong?"

"I'll tell you all about it, Paige. I'll pick you up in ten minutes."

"Okay. Bye."

Robin hung up and quickly changed her clothes. After she had brushed her hair, she ran downstairs. Her parents had come home. Dr. Thomas Anderson was in his study, reading a medical journal. Mrs. Edna Anderson sat in front of the television in the living room. Robin winced when she realized she wouldn't be able to get out of the house without facing them.

"Is that you, Robby?" her father called.

He came out of the study. Dr. Anderson was

tall, lean and angular, with blondish hair that showed signs of gray. He was the most respected surgeon in Port City, a pillar of the community—only his daughter wasn't in the mood to talk to him.

He smiled. "Robby. You were napping when we got home."

Mrs. Anderson poked her head into the hallway. "Is that you, Robin? Would you like some dinner?"

Robin shook her head. "No thanks. I'm late for the hockey game. I have to go."

Mr. Anderson nodded approvingly. "Very well. You know your curfew is eleven on Friday nights."

"Sure, Dad."

Mrs. Anderson, a lovely, blond-haired woman of forty-three, winked at Robin. "Going to see Skip play?"

Robin sighed. "Yeah, Mom. I have to go."

Her father's face tightened with a concerned expression. "Robby, is everything all right? You seem distraught."

"I'm okay, Dad. I just have to—"

"Is everything okay between you and Skip?" her mother asked. "You know you can talk to us—"

Why did they always encourage her to talk? The last thing a teenager wanted was to talk to her parents about important matters like boyfriends and going steady. And, *breaking up!*

Dr. Anderson had no intention of making it any easier. "You know we just adore Skip, honey. Why, when he gave you that ring, your mother almost cried."

Robin's eyes grew wide. "Why is everyone always talking about that damned ring!"

She darted past them, running from the house. The snowfall had accumulated some, but her car wasn't snowed in. She backed out of the driveway and headed for Paige's. Paige lived in town, on the way to Central.

I've been such a fool, Robin thought. *I've let him take everything away from me. How could I have been so stupid?*

Tears formed in her eyes. She had to turn on the windshield wipers to knock the snow from the glass. Port City seemed so dark and forlorn in this snowfall.

As she passed under a street lamp, the yellow-orange light reflected on the ring. *The ring.* Skip thought it made her his property. Her parents expected *the ring* to ensure her happiness forever. *The ring* meant something to everyone except Robin!

Paige was waiting by the window. As soon as Robin pulled up in front of the house on Washington Street, Paige came out and hurried over the walkway as fast as the snow would let her.

"Looks like some snow," Paige said as she climbed into the car. "Hey, how are you, Anderson?"

Robin immediately began to cry.

"Hey," Paige said. "What—"

Robin threw her arms around Paige, hugging her. "It's awful, Paige. It's just terrible."

Paige patted Robin on the back. "Hey, come on. It can't be that bad. Unless you're pregnant or something."

Robin drew back quickly. "No!" She wiped her eyes.

Paige said, "Wow, for a minute there, I thought you and Skip had made a big mistake."

"Skip *was* a big mistake," Robin replied. "But not like you think."

Paige nodded. "I wondered how long it would last."

Robin gawked at her. "You did?"

"Sure. I mean, everyone thinks Skip is a real cool guy, but I could see right through him."

"How?" Robin demanded.

Paige bit her lip. "Robin, you don't want to hear this. I mean, you and Skip have been going out for over a year."

"I want to hear it," Robin replied. "Don't hold back."

"All right, you asked for it. Skip is a conceited, arrogant, self-centered jerk who doesn't really care about you except for how you fit into his life."

Robin laughed a little. "Wow, you really do know him."

"You're not very happy, are you?"

"No, Paige. He tries to control everything I do. He doesn't want me to have any life of my own. And this ring—" She held it up for Paige. "He thinks this stupid ring means that he can tell me what to do all the time."

"It is pretty nice," Paige offered. "Maybe you two are going through a rough time."

Robin shook her head emphatically. "No. It's more than that. A lot more."

"Wow," Paige said. "Sounds like you're heading for the big breakup."

Robin hung her head. "I—maybe—"

Paige took a deep breath. "Oh, Robin, that'd be cool. We could be friends again. Hank really misses you.'"

Hank was Paige's boyfriend.

"I don't know if I can do it," Robin said. "I want to—but I don't know how."

Paige leaned back in the seat. "Well, you could start by not going to the hockey game."

Robin's expression changed suddenly, coming to life, glowing. "The hockey game!"

She put the car in gear and pulled away from the curb.

"But, Robin," Paige told her, "Skip will be at the arena."

"I know, Paige. I know."

Robin didn't care about Skip.

Skip would be on the ice.

And hopefully, Danny Kovack would be in the stands, waiting for Robin to show up.

FIVE

Danny stood at the window of Doreen's Taylor Street apartment, gazing out at the snowfall. He had tried to talk Doreen into going to the hockey game at the arena, but she had whined so badly that he had given up on the idea. Maybe it was for the best. After all, what did he really have in common with those Prescott kids?

"Danny?"

He glanced back over his shoulder. "Yeah?"

Doreen lay on the couch, covered by a thick quilt. They had finished watching the video. Doreen smiled, a thick-lipped grin with smeared lipstick. She had dark hair, black eyes and a pale complexion. Danny thought she wasn't too bad-looking, at least until he compared her to Robin.

"Come over here and kiss me," Doreen said.

Danny sighed. "Not right now." He looked out the window again, wondering why he couldn't get Robin out of his thoughts.

Doreen got off the sofa and came toward him wrapped in the quilt. "What's wrong?"

"Nothing," Danny replied.

She touched his shoulder. "Hey, why don't we sit on the couch for a while?"

He shook his head. "I'm not in the mood anymore, Doreen."

She began to pout. "What's wrong with you? You were hot-to-trot earlier tonight."

Danny didn't reply. He kept seeing Robin's face in his mind. Why did he want the one he couldn't have?

"Danny!"

"Leave me alone, Doreen."

She pushed at him. "You jerk!"

Danny turned back to look at her. "Doreen, I'm just in a mood, okay? You have your moods."

"I don't get like this," she replied. "You won't tell me what's wrong. Is it me?"

No, it's me.

And the blond girl who won't leave my head.

"Danny!"

He took a deep breath. "I'm kind of hungry, Doreen."

"I don't have much here," she replied.

"Why don't we go to Billie's?" he suggested.

Billie's was an old diner car that was located on a side street off Market Square. The place stayed open until midnight on weekends, even when it snowed. There'd be a crowd there at Billie's, kids eating hot dogs and hamburgers.

Doreen frowned. "Billie's?"

"Sure, why not? We can stand in the snow and eat something."

Doreen put her hands on her hips. "I suppose we have to take my car?"

She had picked him up at his father's place after dark. It was too nasty to ride his motorcycle. At least Doreen's old Ford had snow tires.

Danny grimaced. "No, Doreen, we don't have to take your car. I could walk by myself."

She softened a little. "I have to get dressed. Put on some jeans or something."

"Knock yourself out."

She put her hands on his shoulders. "Are you sure it's not me, Danny? I mean—"

He pushed her hands away. "No, it's not you, Doreen."

Danny looked out the window, watching the snowfall.

It's the blond girl, he thought, *the one that's in my head.*

And in my heart.

Robin and Paige sat in the stands of Municipal Arena, gazing toward the icy rink. The game was tied at three-all with two minutes left to play. The crowd cheered for Central, focused on the close match with Dover High. Everyone sat on the edge of their seats, except for Robin and Paige.

Robin kept looking around, searching the stands. Danny hadn't shown yet. And Robin was bummed.

Paige patted her shoulder. "It's okay."

"Why didn't he come?" Robin asked.

"I don't know. Maybe it's the snow. He rides that motorcycle, you know. He probably stayed home."

Robin sighed deeply. "I wish he had come."

She had told Paige all about her attraction to Danny. Paige wasn't sure she approved—after all, it was like jumping from one trouble guy to another. But she didn't want to be judgmental. Robin needed a friend right now, not someone to harp on her about making a big mistake.

"You really think he's cute?" Paige asked.

"Yeah, sort of. I mean, it's not the way he looks. He's got—I don't know—a certain quality. I mean, look at Hank. He isn't the greatest-looking guy."

Paige nodded. "I suppose."

"I'm sorry," Robin replied. "I didn't mean to put Hank down, but looks aren't everything. If they were, I'd still be all gah-gah over Skip."

They focused on the game for a moment. Candy Reed sat in the front row, cheering for Skip. Maybe she deserved to be with Skip, Robin thought. Let Candy find out what a domineering jerk Skip could be.

On the ice, Skip drove toward the Dover goal, faking to his right and then slapping the puck into the net. The arena erupted with cheers. Robin and Paige stayed in their seats, unable to catch the infectious spirit of victory.

Robin glanced around one more time as the buzzer sounded to end the game. Danny had blown her off. Maybe he had wanted to avoid another confrontation with Skip.

Paige nudged her. "Look."

Skip's teammates had hoisted him on their shoulders. As they passed Robin and Paige, Skip waved to them. Robin knew what was expected of her. She had to go to the locker-room door and wait for Skip to come out. Then she had to fawn all over him, tell him that he had played great.

"What now?" Paige asked.

"I have to wait for Skip. Please, come with me."

"All right, but if he gets obnoxious, I'm going to find another ride home."

Robin grabbed her arm. "No! I mean, I don't want to be alone with him. Please—"

"Robin, are you going to break up with him *tonight*?"

"I—I don't know, Paige. I just don't want to be alone with Skip. Not right now."

"Okay, okay. I'll go."

They found their way through the crowd, waiting for Skip at the entrance of the locker room.

Robin's hands were trembling. "I wish Danny had come."

Paige shook her head. "No, Robin. If you're going to end it with Skip, you have to do it regardless of what you feel for any other guy. You have to be strong."

Robin knew that Paige was right. It was still difficult, though. Skip wasn't going to give up without a fight, not after a whole year together.

"What am I going to say?" Robin asked.

"How about 'I'm breaking up with you, Skip,'" Paige replied. "That would do it."

"He's going to go ballistic," Robin offered. "He—"

"He's coming out of the locker room," Paige said. "There he is. Get tough, girl."

Skip swaggered toward them, carrying his hockey gear. He grinned until he saw Paige. Then his eyes narrowed and his face flashed the disapproving scowl that Robin hated.

"Hi, Paige," Skip said in a flippant tone, "I didn't know we were going to have company tonight."

He's going to make this easy, Robin thought.

"I haven't seen Paige for a while," Robin said. "We sat together at the game."

Skip's chest puffed out. "Hey, did I play great or what? The game winner, eh! Now we'll have home ice all through the playoffs. State champs, I can feel it."

Robin looked away, no longer impressed by his bragging. He was just another jock, in love with himself. She didn't really matter. She was simply someone to be controlled, someone to stand by his side while he grabbed all the glory.

"Did you show Paige the ring?" he asked.

Paige folded her arms, nodding absently. "Yes, I saw it."

Skip grinned again. "So, what do you think? Pretty nice, eh? Me and Robin are going to make it permanent one day."

Robin bit her lip, embarrassed by his bravado. She had to end it. No matter how painful it might be, she had to say good-bye to Skip.

Skip's face tightened into the scowl when he noticed their aloofness. "Robin, can I talk to you alone for a minute?"

Paige blushed. "Uh, I can find a ride home."

"Great," Skip replied.

Paige started to move away.

Robin grabbed her arm. "No! I'll take you home, Paige. Just wait for me."

"All right," Paige rejoined. "I'll wait."

She stepped to the other side of the corridor.

Skip's face had grown red with anger. "Why'd you bring her to the game?"

"She's my best friend," Robin told him. "At least she used to be before—"

"She's a bad influence on you," Skip said. "I don't like you hanging out with her."

Robin felt a tightness in her chest. "Skip, you can't tell me who to hang out with. I can make my own decisions."

He made a growling noise and then put his hands on her shoulders. "Look, I'm not in the mood to fight. Some of the guys and me are going to Billie's for food. Why don't you drop Paige at home and meet us there?"

Robin said heatedly, "Oh yeah. It's okay for you to have your friends along, but I can't bring Paige."

"Hey, just to show you what a great guy I am, bring Paige with you," Skip said.

Robin wanted to slap him for being a jerk, but she resisted. Some of Skip's teammates called to him. Skip winked at Robin and told her to meet him at Billie's. When he tried to kiss her on the lips, Robin turned her head to let him brush her cheek.

Skip's upper lip curled. "I'm gonna have to straighten you out, babe. You're gonna get it."

"Just go," Robin told him.

When Skip had joined his friends, Robin walked over to Paige. "He wants to go to Billie's."

Paige made a face. "He's full of himself."

"He's full of something else too! Paige, I'm going to do it. Tonight."

"So we're going to Billie's?"

Robin nodded. "Yes. And I'm breaking off with Skip. I have to."

They left the building, trudging through the snow to Robin's car. The streets had been plowed enough to allow an easy route to Billie's. A crowd had already started to gather outside the wagon-shaped structure. Robin parked the car and then walked with Paige toward the gang of hungry kids who stood in the snow.

She was wondering what she would say to Skip, at least until a familiar face caught her eye.

Robin stopped on the sidewalk. "Look!"

Paige gazed into the crowd. "What?"

"It's Danny Kovack," Robin replied. "And he's with a girl."

Paige shuddered. Skip was on the way with his friends. They'd all be here in a minute.

"There's going to be trouble," Paige said.

But Robin didn't hear her. She was too busy studying Danny Kovack. And the rough-looking girl who stood at Danny's side.

SIX

Danny stiffened when he saw Robin approaching but his face broke into a smile. Doreen, who leaned against Danny, noticed the change in his expression. She followed his eyes to the statuesque blond-haired girl who had stopped on the sidewalk.

"Danny!"

"Huh?"

"Danny, why are you staring at that girl?"

He snapped out of his trance for a moment. "Uh, she's in my English class at school."

Doreen didn't like the way Danny was looking at this blond. Danny had never looked that way at *her*! Doreen glared at the newcomer, wishing that Robin would go away.

Danny waved. "Hey, Robin, over here."

Robin smiled and leaned over to whisper to Paige. "Here goes!"

"Earth to Robin," Paige replied. "Don't you remember? Your soon-to-be ex-boyfriend is on the way."

"I don't care," Robin replied. "Come on, let's talk to them. I want to size up the competition."

They strolled toward Danny and the dark-haired girl. Robin gave Doreen an up-and-down look. Teased hair, too much makeup, pudgy, cheap. Robin couldn't feel jealous, not with the way Danny smiled at her.

"Hi," she said to Danny.

He nodded. "Hey. How was the game?"

"Central won," Robin replied.

"Whoopee!" Doreen said sarcastically "Aren't you little high school girls out late tonight? I mean, isn't it past your bedtime? Maybe you should go home and let Mommy tuck you in."

Robin and Paige ignored her. Paige kept looking for Skip. Her stomach churned in anticipation of Skip's arrival.

"So," Robin said, "what time do you want to get together so we can study?"

Danny shrugged. "I don't know. How about Sunday?"

Doreen bristled. "I thought we were going out on Sunday."

Danny gave her a sidelong look of disapproval. "Doreen, I have to graduate."

She chortled derisively. "Yeah? Well, I blew off high school and I'm doing all right."

Robin offered a catty smile. "Danny isn't doing too well in English. I have to help him."

"I'll bet that's not all you'll help him with," Doreen replied. "Look, you little girls better order something. Danny and I have some things to talk about."

She grabbed Danny's arm and tried to pull him away.

Danny jerked out of her grasp. "Doreen, take a pill. These are my friends from school."

"This is Paige," Robin said quickly.

"Hi," Paige said, though she did not look at Danny. Paige kept scanning the crowd. Why hadn't the hockey boys arrived yet?

"How about Sunday at one o'clock?" Robin offered.

"Okay," Danny replied.

Doreen grabbed his arm again. "You promised to take me to the movies on Sunday."

"No, I didn't," Danny said.

Robin was secretly thrilled that Danny preferred her to the girl at his side. She wasn't jealous of Doreen. She certainly had no right to be; after all, she was still going steady with Skip—technically. But that would all change in a hurry.

Robin kept smiling at Danny. "If you can't ride your motorcycle, I can pick you up."

"I bet you can!" Doreen quipped.

Paige's eyes grew wide. "Robin—"

But Robin's smile had changed into a look of anger. "What's your problem, Doreen?"

"Robin," Paige persisted, tugging at her sleeve.

Doreen glared at Robin. "Look, little girl, why don't you take your bouncy blond hair somewhere else?"

"It's a free country," Robin replied. "I can talk to Danny if I want to."

"Robin," Paige said frantically, "I think you'd better cool it. Look who's coming."

But Robin had locked eyes with Doreen and she wasn't backing off one inch.

Doreen's eyes narrowed. "Look, little girl, you'd better watch it or you might get your face ripped off!"

Paige jerked Robin to the side. "Robin, look—"

"Huh?"

Danny glared into the crowd. "Great. The no-necks are here."

"What the hell is going on?" Skip blared through the frigid air. "Robin, why are you talking to these skanks?"

Robin turned quickly to regard Skip and the four friends that flanked him. They were all scowling at Danny. Everyone in the crowd had taken notice of Skip's entrance. Now they had focused on the confrontation that was brewing.

Doreen shot a nasty look at Skip. "Hey, butthead, who you calling a skank?"

Robin almost laughed. For a moment she appreciated Doreen's spirit. Nobody ever talked to Skip like that.

Doreen waved with her hand, like she was brushing crumbs from a kitchen table. "Why don't you little birds just fly on home and get Mommy to make you some cookies?"

Skip bristled, not sure how to reply.

Paige leaned toward Robin. "We have to get out of this. We can't let them fight."

One of Skip's buddies shot back. "That's Doreen the mattress queen. She dropped out of Central when my brother was a senior."

"Yeah," another voice rejoined, "I heard she went steady with the football team."

Danny finally spoke up. "Put a lid on it, crew cut. You can't talk to her like that."

Skip met Danny's hostile gaze. "You'd better leave now, hood, or you're gonna get hurt."

Robin glanced back and forth between them, wondering if Skip and Danny would fight. She couldn't believe that they would square off over her. If they did, she wanted Danny to kick Skip's backside.

"Stop them," Paige urged.

Robin shook her head. "Let it happen."

Skip took a step toward Danny. "You'd better make like a banana and split, biker-boy."

"Or what?" Danny replied. "The five of you will jump me? That takes a lot of guts, Chesterton. Five against one. What's the matter? You afraid to face me alone? One on one."

Skip's face slacked at the challenge. "I'm not afraid of you, Kovack. You name the time and place."

Doreen tugged at Danny's sleeve. "Come on, let's blow this place, Danny. I don't want any trouble with the cops."

"You should take the skank's advice," Skip blurted out.

Danny crooked his finger, motioning for Skip to come closer. "Let's do it, jock. You take the first swing. Come on, let all your buddies watch you get your butt kicked."

"Do it, Skip," one of his friends said.

"Yeah, kick that greaser's teeth in."

"You can do it, Skip."

Danny grinned. "Yeah, you can do it, Skip. Let's party."

Skip hesitated. "Look, there's no need for trouble."

"That ship has sailed," Danny replied. "You started it, now do you want to finish it or what?"

"This isn't the place," Skip said.

Danny nodded toward Doreen. "Then you can apologize to the lady before you leave."

"Don't apologize to that skank, Skip!"

"Yeah, she's a *ho*!"

"Punch his lights out, Skip."

Skip glanced back over his shoulder. "Shut up!"

"Big man on the ice," Danny taunted. "You ain't much without a stick in your hand."

Skip looked at Robin. "Come on, Robin, we're out of here right now."

Robin scoffed at him. "No way, Skip. I'm getting a hot dog and a cup of hot chocolate."

"What?" Skip asked with a tone of incredulity.

"Maybe you'd better go with him," Paige urged. "Before he loses it completely."

Skip pointed a finger at Robin. "Listen to her. You could be making a big mistake, Robin. That ring—"

Robin scowled back at him. "Screw *that ring*!" she cried. "I'm so sick of hearing about that damned ring!"

Skip's jaw dropped. "Hey—"

Robin pulled the ring from her finger and threw it at him. "Take it and shove it, Skip."

The ring landed at his feet in the snow.

"Wow," Paige muttered. "Heavy drama."

"She can't get away with that," one of the hockey goons bellowed.

"Yeah, Skip, show her who's boss."

"She can't do that to you!"

Skip reached down, plucking the ring from the snow. "Robin, you don't know what you're saying."

"I sure as hell do," Robin replied. "I'm breaking up with you, Skip. It's over. Finished!"

"But the ring—"

"I never asked for the ring. I liked it at first, but then you started treating me like a dog. I'm not a dog, Skip. I'm a human being."

Skip focused his hate-filled eyes on Paige. "You! You talked her into this! It's all your fault."

Paige chortled nervously. "Me? No, it wasn't me, Skip. It was you. You're the one who acts so possessive."

When Skip looked at Robin again, his face softened into a frown of agony. "Robin, please. Don't do this. I can change. I can do better. We'll talk. I—I love you."

Robin sighed, shaking her head, unmoved by his pleas. "Well, Skip, I don't love you! You're a jerk and I'm glad I'm breaking up with you."

For a moment everything was quiet. Skip glared at Danny, bristling, ready to fight. Then something totally unexpected happened. The crowd began to applaud. Cheers egged Robin on. Apparently, Skip's only friends were the four goons who flanked him.

Skip started toward Danny. "You and me, creep!"

Danny tensed, pushing Doreen away. "You got it, jock."

But before Skip reached him, a bright light flashed in their faces. "What's going on here!" a loudspeaker blared.

Skip stopped in the snow. A Port City police cruiser had pulled up to the snack wagon. One of the officers got out with his hand on his nightstick.

"There's no trouble, Officer," Paige said quickly. "Everything is all right. Skip and his friends were just leaving. Weren't you, Skip?"

Skip deflated, faking a smile. "Uh, yeah. No trouble, sir. I was just telling my friend Danny here how I'd see him later."

"Cool," Danny replied. "You know where to find me—*friend*!"

Skip shot one last hostile look at Robin before he turned and stormed off with his friends.

The police officer lingered for a moment, flashing the light in Danny's eyes. "We're gonna be watching you, Kovack."

"Thank you," Danny replied. "I appreciate it, sir."

The officer grimaced and muttered, "Punk."

He climbed back into the squad car and the cruiser rolled down the street into the snowy night.

Robin shuddered. "Well, that was intense."

Danny smiled at her. "Yeah, really."

Their eyes met.

She had really broken up with Skip.

And Robin could tell by the sparkle in Danny's eyes that he cared about her.

Doreen saw the look and she wasn't too happy about it.

Paige wasn't happy either. She was nervous. She had to wonder what would happen now that Skip had been dumped. Skip wasn't the type to let things rest. Paige was almost certain that he would retaliate. She just wasn't sure how or when Skip would strike.

SEVEN

By the time Doreen and Danny left Billie's, the snowfall had slacked off to flurries. Doreen sat behind the wheel of the car, staring blankly ahead at the dark street. She wasn't happy about the way Danny had paid so much attention to the blond-haired girl from Central Academy. Doreen had never liked silver-spoon, cream-cheese types like Robin. They thought they were better than everyone else.

Danny sat on the passenger side, half smiling. He kept thinking about the way Skip had backed down. Of course, the cops had prompted part of Skip's retreat, but Danny knew the hockey jock was afraid of him. Skip, and his kind, never fought without a whole gang of friends for backup.

Doreen made the turn to go to her place.

"Where are you taking me?" Danny asked.

She shrugged. "To my house."

He shook his head. "No, take me home."

Doreen's face tightened into a vicious scowl. "Oh, I see, meetin' your little hot potato for a midnight snack."

Danny grimaced and looked out the window. "Doreen—"

"Don't think I don't know what's goin' on, Kovack! You've got it bad for that little tramp. I can see it. And she's got it bad for you."

Danny smiled and looked at Doreen. "Yeah? You really think she likes me?"

"Gee, I don't know," Doreen said in a mocking tone. "Maybe I can pass her a note in gym class."

Danny leaned back on the seat, peering at the flurries. Robin *did* care about him. Doreen had confirmed it and Danny was inclined to believe her because girls picked up on stuff like that.

Doreen drove on, stopping in front of the old apartment house where she lived. "I'm home."

"But I—"

She glared at him. "If you don't want to stay here, then you can just walk!"

Doreen got out of the car, slamming the door behind her. She stormed up the walk to the front steps. At the entrance to the building, she hesitated, looking back to see if Danny was going to follow her.

Danny opened the car door and stepped onto the street. He didn't even look at Doreen. He just started walking away, moving along the snow-laced avenue. With Robin swirling in his head, he couldn't even think of a girl like Doreen. Not that there was anything wrong with Doreen—she just wasn't Robin.

"That's right!" Doreen cried. "Go on. You'll be back. You hear me? You'll be back!"

Danny barely heard her threats. It wasn't a long walk to the waterfront, but the cold wind made it seem longer. When he reached the diner, he went upstairs to hear his father's snoring. Old Lazlo was down for the count.

Danny flopped on his bed, gazing up at the ceiling.

The word formed on his lips like a prayer. "Robin."

Did he really have a chance with her?

Or was he just fooling himself?

No, it was there, the sparkle in her eyes.

He had a real shot with the blond-haired girl.

For the first time in his life, Danny Kovack allowed himself to be careless with hope.

Robin steered the Escort toward Prescott

Estates. Paige sat on the passenger side, gazing out the window. It had been quite an evening. Robin had asked Paige to stay over, so they could talk about what had happened.

"Did you see the look on Skip's face?" Robin asked triumphantly. "He was pee-ohed!"

Paige still felt nervous about Skip and possible retaliation. "You embarrassed him, Robin. In front of everyone."

"He had it coming," Robin replied. "He's been pushing my buttons for a whole year."

Paige shook her head. "I don't know, Robin. Skip could do something that you wouldn't like."

"Like what?" Robin challenged. "He's a wimp."

"He may get his boys to beat up Danny."

Robin shook her head. "No way. Skip's a wuss. He won't do anything. Wow, did you see the way I threw that ring at him?"

"Yes, I did," Paige replied.

Robin laughed. "And they say breaking up is hard to do. It was great!"

Paige wasn't so sure. Skip had really been humiliated. Was Skip capable of something drastic? Paige figured he wouldn't take it lying down. Although what finally happened would be a big surprise to everyone at Central Academy.

"Robin, honey, would you and Danny like some hot chocolate?"

Mrs. Anderson stood at the archway of the living room, gazing at Robin and her new "friend." Dr. Anderson had also scrutinized the boy who Robin was tutoring. Danny Kovack looked a bit rougher than Robin's other friends, but her parents were willing to give her the benefit of the doubt.

Robin looked up from a text of English poetry. "Uh, I don't care for any, Mom. How about you, Danny?"

Danny smiled warmly. "Uh, sure, I'd love some, Mrs. Anderson."

Her mother nodded and went back into the kitchen.

"Your mom is great," Danny said. "A real mom who makes hot chocolate and everything. It's cool."

Robin blushed. "You think so?"

"Yeah, I lost my mother. She died of cancer a couple of years ago. It was pretty tough."

"Oh, I'm sorry."

Danny sighed. "So, how does this poetry thing work?"

"It doesn't *work*," Robin replied. "You read the words and make what you can out of it."

"Oh."

The Sunday tutoring session hadn't gone too badly, Robin thought. Danny had good reading skills, he just wasn't trained in analyzing poetry. It might take a lot of sessions for him to catch on, which would give Robin an excuse to spend more time with him.

Mrs. Anderson reentered the room. "Hot chocolate for you, Danny. With marshmallows."

"Thank you, Mrs. Anderson."

Her mother lingered for a moment. "So, Robin, have you heard from Skip today?"

Robin grimaced. "Uh, no, Mom. Skip and I broke up."

Edna Anderson raised an eyebrow. "Really? You seem to be taking it very well."

"I am," Robin replied.

"How's Skip taking it?" Mrs. Anderson asked.

"Mom!"

Danny smiled. "It's okay. I wonder how he *is* taking it?"

Robin hadn't heard from Skip since the breakup on Friday night. The phone hadn't rung. He hadn't tried to reach her.

How *was* Skip dealing with the dissolution of their relationship?

Robin felt elated, though Paige had warned her about all the worst possible scenarios.

But they wouldn't really know how Skip was doing until he approached Robin and Danny on Monday in the Central Academy cafeteria.

Robin, Paige and Danny were sitting to-

gether in the lunchroom when Skip entered
with his friends. Danny straightened immediately, anticipating trouble. Robin had gone
the better part of the Monday without as
much as seeing Skip. But now Skip stood on
the other side of the cafeteria, peering at
Robin with a forlorn look on his handsome
face. Candy stood beside him, glaring at
Robin. Candy had already moved in to pick
the bones.

"Great," Paige muttered. "An instant re-
play of Friday night at Billie's."

Danny grimaced. "Damn. I don't want to
fight him here. I don't want to get kicked out
of school."

Robin bit her lip. "Uh, I don't think he's
going to come over here. Not now."

"Guess again," Danny replied.

Paige made a face. "Uh-oh."

Skip left his friends, walking across the
cafeteria to the table where Robin sat with
Danny and Paige.

What was he going to do?

As soon as Skip reached the table, Danny
rose quickly.

Skip held up his palms. "Take it easy,
Kovack. Okay? I'm not here to cause trouble."

Danny's eyes narrowed. "You're not?"

Robin gaped at Skip, not ready to trust
him. "What's up, Skip? What do you want
from us?"

A pained expression came and went on Skip's countenance. He tried to brace himself. What he had to say would not come easy.

"Uh, Robin," Skip started. "I'm sorry that I was so rude on Friday night."

Danny eased down again, sitting at the table. "Sorry?"

Skip nodded. "Yeah, I'm sorry, Kovack. And, Paige. I didn't see it coming. I didn't realize that Robin hated me so much."

Robin sighed. "I don't hate you, Skip. I just didn't want to go steady anymore."

Skip closed his eyes for a moment before he looked at her and spoke in a trembling voice. "I know, Robin. But I want to be a good guy about all this. I don't want you to hate me. And I don't want you to think I'm going to threaten you, Danny. I had time to think, and I'm accepting all this the best I can."

Robin nodded toward Candy. "Looks like you have some help."

Paige nudged her. "Robin—"

"No, it's okay," Skip replied. "Candy is a good friend. She's helping me to get through all this. She said I should square things with you, see if we can still be friends."

Robin sighed. "Friends?"

"You know," Skip offered, "just be nice to each other."

Robin shrugged. "Why not?"

Skip looked at Danny. "No hard feelings, Kovack?" He extended his hand.

Danny shook hands with Skip. "No hard feelings, Chesterton."

Skip glanced at Robin again. "So, are you and Kovack going together now?"

Danny quickly glanced away. "Uh, she's just helping me with my English, Skip."

So far!

Robin tired to keep from getting mad. "Skip, that's really none of your business."

Paige looked into her lunch tray, not saying a word.

Skip held up his hands. "Hey, I'm sorry. Look, I'll see you later. Okay? I'm outta here."

He turned and walked back to his friends.

Paige whistled. "Wow. He took that better than I thought."

Danny chortled. "I didn't think he had it in him."

Robin shrugged off Skip's apology. "Who cares? It's over."

She looked at Danny, grinning.

He smiled back at her.

It was great, Robin thought.

Everything was going to be all right.

Just not forever.

EIGHT

"I love you, Danny," Robin said. "I love you with all my heart and soul."

She gazed into his dark eyes, smiling. Danny wore a grim expression on his face. He touched her shoulders, gently pushing her away from him.

"What's wrong?" Robin asked.

Danny shook his head. "We're wrong, Robin. It can't work. I don't love you."

"No! You're lying, Danny. You do love me. I know it. I can see it in your eyes."

He turned his back to her. "You're wrong. We just aren't right for each other."

Robin grabbed Danny, turning him toward her. She looked into his eyes, but they were no longer there. The sockets were empty. Danny's eyes had simply disappeared.

"No!"

Danny started to laugh. "I can't see you, Robin!"

She stepped back, trying to retreat. She bumped into someone. Robin wheeled to see Skip standing there. He had no eyes, just like Danny. And he was also laughing.

"You blew it!" Skip cried. "I was the best. But you blew me off for Kovack!"

"No," Robin insisted. "I—"

"He doesn't want you," Skip went on in a horrible voice. "You aren't good enough for a hood from Pitney Docks!"

Robin tried to run from him, but there were more eyeless creatures everywhere. Paige stood there, Skip's friends, Candy Reed. They all laughed at her, staring with the dark sockets where their eyeballs should've been.

A circle formed around Robin. The blind creatures moved in to tighten the ring. Suddenly their hands extended, showing long, sharp claws.

"We want your blood, Robin!"

"Blood!" Danny cried.

"No! Please—"

Their voices chimed in harmony, gradually transforming into a dull, bleating noise that rescued Robin from the dream.

Robin sat up in her bed, sweating and trying to catch her breath. It was the second time she had suffered through the horrid vision. What did it mean? Why were they after her?

The telephone next to her bed kept ringing. "Hello?"

"Hey, it's Paige. Are you awake?"

Robin sighed. "Yeah, I just opened my eyes." She shuddered, wondering if she should tell Paige about the dream.

"How about a ride to school today?" Paige asked.

"Okay."

The vision had seemed so real.

"Robin, did you talk to Danny about the Valentine's Day Dance at the country club?"

"Uh, yeah. Paige, let me get ready. I'll pick you up in a half hour."

"Okay, see ya."

Robin hung up. She had been thinking about how to ask Danny to the Valentine's Day Dance, which was only eight days away. She wanted Danny as her date, but she wasn't sure he would want to go to the country club. Skip and Candy would be there, along with a lot of the other kids whose parents could afford to pay dues to Port City's most exclusive organization.

As Robin staggered through her morning routine, the heavy feeling of the nightmare would not leave her. Why had the dream come two nights in a row? Things had been fine between her and Danny—so far.

For nearly a month, Robin had continued to tutor Danny, which accounted for his English grade rising to a C+. Robin hoped Danny could pull a B for the final mark. They had until June to work on it.

Robin gazed at her reflection in the mirror. She had been spending a lot of time with Danny, but the relationship had not progressed the way she desired. They had grown closer, had become good friends, but except for a couple of lukewarm pecks on the cheek, Danny hadn't made a move on her.

That's why I'm having the dream, she thought. *He doesn't really love me.*

Yet, he called her all the time and spent every moment with her that he could find. Danny had opened up to Robin, telling her all about his rough childhood, the loss of his mother, the sister who had run away from home never to be heard from again. He had confessed that he had saved three thousand dollars toward his college education, that he planned to attend Port City Community College for the first two years.

He loves me.

He loves me not.

She had played the game as a little girl, pulling the petals from wild daisies.

If he doesn't love me, why does he spend so much time with me?

She sighed and turned away from the mir-

ror. The country club dance would be the
telltale indicator. If Danny accepted her invi-
tation to the dance, she'd know how he really
felt.

When she was dressed for the winter day,
she went downstairs and drank some orange
juice. Her mother tired to get her to eat some
eggs, but Robin only grabbed a piece of dry
toast and hurried out to her car. Another
snowfall had left high banks of white on the
streets and yards of Port City. Robin cranked
up the Escort and drove slowly through the
narrow streets until she reached Paige's
house. Paige waited by the window as usual.

"I'm sick of winter," Paige said as she
climbed into the car. "How about you?"

Robin shrugged. "I guess."

Paige glanced sideways at her. "It's Danny,
isn't it?"

Robin nodded. "Yes, it's Danny."

Paige bit her lip and looked out the window. She hadn't been negative about Robin's
relationship with Danny, but she hadn't been
enthusiastic either. Robin had obviously noticed.

Skip had been great about the breakup.
Every time Skip saw Robin with Danny, he
smiled and waved at them. Skip and Candy
had been getting along well. Everyone
seemed to be happy. Still, Paige wasn't sure

about the change. Somehow, the events of the past month had been unsettling.

"I want to ask Danny to the country club dance," Robin offered. "But I don't know how."

Paige frowned. "The Valentine's Day Dance?"

Robin nodded. "I'm afraid Danny will refuse to go with me. It's not his scene."

"Robin, maybe you and Danny aren't right for each other."

"I know he cares," Robin replied. "And I really care about him. I've never met anyone like Danny. He's different."

Paige sighed. "I don't know—"

Robin glanced quickly at Paige. "You don't approve of me going out with Danny, do you?"

"Robin—"

"Be truthful, Paige, I can take it. I mean, you are my best friend. Danny hasn't messed that up the way Skip did. Danny has been wonderful, a perfect gentleman."

"I know, Robin. And I'm not going to say anything bad about Danny. But the country club Valentine's Dance? Do you really think he'll want to go."

"I hope so. And if he doesn't, we can do something else. I don't care about that dance anyway."

"You don't?" Paige challenged.

"All right, I care!" Robin replied quickly. "The Valentine's Dance is important to me."

"Why?"

"Because I want to show everyone that Danny isn't just a motorcycle-riding punk. He's a very intelligent and sensitive person who deserves their respect."

Paige admired Robin for standing up for the boy she cared so much about. Maybe Danny *did* belong with Robin. Or maybe he *didn't*.

"All right," Paige said. "You've convinced me. Now ask him."

Robin stiffened behind the wheel. "Okay! I'll ask him right after school."

"Good," Paige replied.

But Paige was thinking, *I hope you know what you're doing.*

When the final bell rang, Robin left the gymnasium and hurried across campus to the senior building. The cold air swirled with light snow flurries that drifted in a brisk breeze. For the entire school day, Robin had been trying to get up the courage to tell Danny about the country club dance.

What if he turned her down?

What if he didn't love her at all?

She entered the senior building, escaping from the snow and the freezing temperatures.

As Robin brushed the flakes from her

shoulder, she heard a familiar voice. "Hey, Robin, how are you?"

Skip and Candy strode toward her. Robin tried to smile at them but her expression was more like a friendly grimace. She still couldn't stand to be around Skip and Candy, even though they had been nice to her all along. She wasn't jealous of them together, she just didn't care enough to hang out with them.

"Hi," Robin said weakly, turning toward her locker to get away from Skip and Candy.

But they were intent on being pleasant, so they followed her in the hall.

"Going to the country club dance?" Skip asked.

"Maybe," Robin replied.

She had to stop at her locker.

Skip and Candy stopped with her.

"The dance is going to be great," Candy offered. "Skip and I are going. I've already picked out my dress. Have you decided what you're going to wear, Robin?"

"No, I haven't, Candy."

She stared into the locker, wishing they would go away.

"Is Danny coming?" Candy asked.

Before Robin could reply, Danny was there, smiling at her. "Hey, Robin. Skip, Candy. What's doing?"

Skip grinned from ear to ear. "We were just

talking about the dance at the country club."

"What dance?" Danny asked, looking at Robin.

Robin started to say something.

But Candy butted in. "The Valentine's Day Dance," she replied. "Hasn't Robin told you?"

Danny's eyes narrowed. "No—"

Robin slammed her locker door. "Come on, Danny." She put her arm through Danny's arm and pulled him away from Skip and Candy.

Danny acted hurt. "What's all this dance stuff?"

"I'll tell you in the car."

When they were sitting in the Escort, Robin braced herself and informed Danny about the country club dance on Valentine's Day.

He sat there listening with a dull look on his face. "Why didn't you tell me about this before? Don't you want me to go?"

Robin grabbed his hand. "Yes, I—I mean, I *do* want you to go. I've dreamed about it. It's just—"

He glared at her with his dark eyes. "Just what?"

"I—I didn't think you'd want to go to a dance at the country club, Danny. I was afraid to ask you. I mean, sometimes you act like you don't care about me."

His eyes grew wide. "Don't care about you?

Robin, I'm crazy about you. I love you more than anyone I've ever known."

Her jaw dropped open. "What?"

"Look, I've been taking it slow," Danny replied. "I didn't want to scare you off. You're not like the other girls I've been with. You've got class. You—"

Robin grabbed him, pressing her lips to his mouth. Danny responded immediately, kissing her back. They kissed for a long time before Danny drew back.

"Wow—"

"I love you, Danny."

He shook his head, whistling. "I love you too. Hey, you think we could kiss like that again?"

Their lips met. Soon, the windows of the Escort were obscured by a light film of fog. Danny broke away again.

"Take it slow," he said. "Okay?"

She laughed. "Most guys want to take it *fast*!"

"So do I," Danny replied. "But you're a classy girl, Robin. I'm not going to be like that with you. I—"

He grabbed her for another kiss.

Robin broke away this time. "All right, are you going to the Valentine's Dance or not?"

Danny grinned. "I'm going. But only if you'll help me pick out a tux."

"You got it, babe."

They couldn't stop themselves from embracing again.

Robin felt herself transported by his kiss. She had never known anything like it. Would it always be this great between them?

It wouldn't.

NINE

The port City Country Club had been festooned with bright, pinpoint lights for the Valentine's Day Dance. The limbs of every bare tree around the clubhouse had been strung with miniature white bulbs, giving the snowy grounds an eerie, almost heavenly glow. The dance was the highlight of midwinter, drawing nearly one hundred percent of the club membership, a true gala affair for the members of Port City's social elite.

The previous year, Robin had attended the dance with Skip. Now she sat in the backseat of her father's Lincoln town car, snuggling up to Danny to escape the February cold. Danny gazed out the window of the car, his eyes wide at the splendor of the club. For a moment he felt like an outsider, but when he looked into

Robin's lovely eyes, everything seemed okay again.

"I love you," she mouthed silently, so her parents wouldn't hear in the front seat.

Danny returned the compliment with a whispered, "I love you too, Robin."

Danny acted so humble, modest, grateful. He had never attended anything like this before. Robin had assisted Danny with picking out the tuxedo and then had showed him how to put it on. She had also urged him to get a new haircut, which made him look even more handsome.

Robin's mother and father hadn't been too excited about her dropping Skip for Danny, though they had not protested. Both of them were watching Danny, waiting for him to make a mistake, to do something untoward so their suspicions would be confirmed. But Danny had not disappointed them in any way. Robin hoped they were starting to accept him.

Dr. Anderson guided the Lincoln under the sheltered entrance of the country club. He stepped out, cutting quite an elegant figure in his evening clothes. Mrs. Anderson, Danny had commented earlier, looked like a movie star in her gown.

When a valet opened the back door for Robin and Danny, Danny remarked, "Cool."

He climbed out and then reached back to give Robin a hand.

Robin couldn't stop smiling as she looked into his face. She had reformed this rough biker, smoothing out his jagged edges. Yet, there was still an undefinable quality about Danny that kept Robin guessing.

Danny shook his head, marveling at the spectacle before him. "It's like Xanadu," he said. "Like in that poem by Coleridge."

Robin smiled at the literary reference. Danny's English was coming right along. He would probably pull a B in the course for the final grade, though Robin was still a little nervous about the impending term paper that every Central student had to write before he or she could graduate.

Dr. Anderson gave a sweeping gesture and then offered his arm to his wife. "Shall we?" he asked in a playful tone.

Edna Anderson feigned regal elegance. "Yes, my lord."

Danny grinned at Robin and then offered his arm. "Shall we?"

Robin took his arm. "By all means."

As soon as they were inside, they checked their overcoats. Danny stood still for a moment, checking his tuxedo. Robin straightened the black bow tie.

"You're going to do fine," she said.

Danny swallowed nervously and tried to

keep his chin up. "What if nobody likes me?" he said. "What if—"

She put her fingers on his lips. "Shh. Do just like we practiced. You're going to be great."

"I hope so."

They followed Robin's parents through an ornate lobby, emerging in the main ballroom of the clubhouse. A live orchestra played a slow-dancing tune, allowing the perfect couples to glide effortlessly over the dance floor. The formal, sit-down dinner would come later, after the celebration.

Danny eyed the dancers with a nervous expression. "Wow, I hope I can remember the two-step you showed me." He was beginning to perspire a little.

"You can do it," Robin whispered.

She was ready to guide him onto the dance floor when a high, lilting and affected voice called Robin's name.

Robin grimaced. "Mrs. Cutshawl."

Danny studied the blue-haired woman who sauntered toward them. "Who is she?"

"The chairman of the Valentine's Dance committee," Robin replied. "She's also a distant cousin of my mother's."

Danny tensed, his first encounter with a true minion of Port City society.

Robin hoped he could handle Mrs. Cutshawl.

"Hello, my dear Robin," Mrs. Cutshawl said effusively. "And who is this handsome young man with you?"

"My name is Daniel Kovack," Danny replied, extending his hand. "So very glad to meet you, Mrs. Cutshawl. You look wonderful tonight."

Yeah, Danny thought, her hair looks like a blue motorcycle helmet with a metal-flake job!

But he was terribly charming and hard to resist. "Why, thank you, Mr. Kovack."

"Call me Danny."

Mrs. Cutshawl glanced at Robin. "Where is your father? I must talk to him immediately."

"I believe he went to the other side of the room," Robin replied. "Yes, there he is."

Mrs. Cutshawl put her hand on Danny's forearm. "Please, save a dance for an old woman, would you, Daniel?"

"I'd be delighted," Danny replied.

Mrs. Cutshawl hurried off to quiz Dr. Anderson about the delightful young man who was dating his daughter.

Robin beamed her approval, grinning at Danny. "Wow, you really did your homework."

Danny shrugged, gaining back some of his cockiness. "Hey, it was all those old movies you made me watch. What was that guy's name, the one you told me to study?"

"Cary Grant," Robin replied.

Danny nodded. "Yeah. Your father has a great video collection. So I'm going for it, Robin. Tonight, the boy leaves Pitney Docks. Care to dance, darling?"

She still could not believe it. "What's gotten into you?"

"I'm bad, baby!"

For a moment she heard the biker calling. But then Danny led her to the dance floor and they twirled in time with the music. Robin had never felt this way in the arms of Skip. How could he do this to her?

She wanted to kiss him right there on the floor, but Robin knew that sort of behavior was unacceptable at the country club.

When the music stopped, Robin and Danny walked off the dance floor with everyone watching them. They were the most handsome couple at the celebration. She led him to the buffet table that was filled with rich appetizers.

"Man, this is great, Robin. I always thought people like this were snobs. But they really seem to like me."

Robin stared into his eyes. "I really like you too, Danny. I've been thinking—"

His expression slacked into a playful frown. "What?"

"Well, are we—I mean, it seems like we're getting along pretty well. Don't you think so?"

"Yeah, I guess."

She fingered the lapels of his tuxedo jacket. "Well, usually when a guy and a girl get together like us, they're going steady."

"Isn't that term a little old-fashioned?" Danny asked.

"Maybe."

She took a deep breath. How was she going to tell him that she thought they should take their relationship a lot further? A step she had never taken before. It was frightening, yet, it was there inside her. What would he think?

"Danny, I—"

"Well, if it isn't my old friend Kovack!"

Danny flinched. "No way," he muttered.

Robin recognized the voice. "Skip. I forgot that he was coming tonight."

Skip slapped Danny on the shoulder and regarded Robin. "Hi, welcome to the country club. Are you guys having a good time?"

"Sure," Danny replied.

Robin nodded. She actually didn't mind seeing Skip. After all, he was pleasant enough and there hadn't been any trouble since the breakup. Skip had simply intruded on what was going to be an ultrapersonal moment between Robin and Danny.

"What do you think of the place?" Skip asked.

Danny nodded, looking around. "Fancy."

Skip leaned closer, whispering, "I hope you

don't feel out of place, Kovack. I mean, these people can be a little stuffy. You know what I mean?"

Danny shrugged. "Well, I had to promise Mrs. Cutshawl a dance, but everything else has been great."

"Skip? There you are!"

Candy came up next to Skip, taking his arm. "Hello, Robin."

Robin could've chipped ice from Candy's voice. She smiled at Candy, showing her that there was no reason to be catty. Robin genuinely wanted everyone to be friends and to get along. She was fairly certain that Skip wanted the same thing, since he was being so nice to them.

Skip put his arm around Candy's shoulder. "My man Danny was just telling me that Mrs. Cutshawl was hitting on him."

Candy laughed. "Really? Well, Danny sure looks good tonight. You've really changed him, Robin."

Danny drew Robin close to him. "Guys, it's official. We're going steady now. Aren't we, honey?"

Robin's face lit up. "Yes, it's great."

Skip nodded approvingly. "This calls for a celebration. Let me get some glasses of punch so we can toast."

"Yes," Candy offered. "Skip and I are going together too. He just asked me yesterday."

"I'm happy for you," Robin said. "I really am."

Skip returned with four champagne glasses filled with red punch. "Here, Danny. You take this one. Candy. And Robin." Skip hoisted his glass. "To the happy couples."

"It all worked out for the best," Robin added.

Candy put in her two cents. "For the best."

Danny clinked his glass. "It's rad to have friends."

Skip downed his glass in one gulp. Danny did the same thing. The toast appeared to wipe out any lingering feelings of uneasiness between the four celebrants. They began to talk effusively, as if they had been old friends forever.

Robin kept watching Danny, who swelled with pride. He became more animated. It was clear he was having a good time. Maybe too good a time.

"Are you okay?" Robin asked when she noticed that the sweat had beaded on his forehead.

"I'm stoked!" Danny replied. "I've never had so much fun in my whole life."

He kissed Robin fully on the mouth, drawing a couple of stares from the older guests.

"Danny, not here," Robin told him.

"Sure, babe. Hey, Chesterton, let's get some more of that punch. Whattaya say?"

Skip and Danny walked off together like they were best buddies.

What had gotten in to him? Robin wondered.

He had been so composed in the beginning.

Maybe it was all going to his head.

Maybe she should have a talk with him.

The change had happened so suddenly.

His movements had become jerky, larger, almost out of control.

Still, Danny seemed to be doing all right.

Until they sat down for the formal dinner.

TEN

Dinner was being served in seven courses to the country club guests. The appetizer had come and gone. Now they were starting on their soup. Robin sat next to Danny, watching him closely. Danny wore a stupid grin on his face as he slurped soup from the bowl.

"Hey, this junk is cold!" Danny said in a loud voice.

Robin leaned over toward him. "Shh. It's french. Cold potato soup."

Danny pushed the bowl away. "It sucks! Soup should be hot, babe. Like you!" He kept grinning.

What was wrong with him? He had been so well mannered before. Had the pressure gotten to him?

"Danny, please," Robin said. "Everyone's looking."

93

"Huh? Oh! Let them look. I don't care."

Sweat poured off Danny's face. His hair was all mussed and his eyes had grown glassy. He yanked at the bow tie until it fell loosely around his neck. Then he unbuttoned his formal shirt, letting the collar flap open.

"Hot," he muttered. "My head. It's spinning. Man, I got a headache."

Robin studied him with narrow eyes. She was beginning to think that she should take Danny home. The country club atmosphere didn't seem to agree with him anymore.

"Danny, are you all right?" she asked.

"Sure, babe. Except for that freakin' cold soup. Hey, can somebody warm it up for me?"

He reached for the bowl, knocking it over. The cold, white liquid spilled on the tablecloth. A waiter appeared immediately to wipe up the mess.

"Excuse me, sir," the waiter said politely.

Danny laughed. "Whoa, did you hear that dude? He called me *sir*! That's really cool."

Robin looked around nervously. More and more of the guests were taking notice of Danny's loud behavior, including her parents. Dr. Anderson stared in their direction with a concerned tilt to his countenance. Mrs. Anderson also glared at Danny.

Skip, who sat on the other side of Robin, leaned over to whisper to her. "What's with Danny?"

"I don't know," Robin replied.

"Want me to get him out of here for you?" Skip asked.

She shook her head. "No, I'll deal with it."

Danny pushed the waiter away from the table. "Go get me some hot soup, dude. That cold crap tastes like freakin'—"

"Danny!" Robin said firmly.

He snapped his head around, peering at her with that glassy expression. "What?"

"Stop acting like this," Robin replied.

"Hey, I ain't actin' like nothin', babe. I'm just havin' a great time. Party down!"

"Danny, everyone is looking at you! Stop it. Now!"

Danny's head turned slowly as he regarded the other guests who were stationed at their tables, eating quietly. Most of them were peering in the direction of the boy who was making so much commotion. They couldn't understand why Robin would bring someone like this to a country club function.

Danny laughed. "Hey, we're all just havin' a good time, babe. Aren't we, Mrs. Cutshawl? Hey, Cuttie baby, lookin' bad with that blue hair. Whoa, radical!"

Across the room, Mrs. Cutshawl turned a vivid shade of red. She spoke to the guests beside her, no doubt casting aspersions on Robin's date. A murmur rose on the air as others began to nod and whisper about Danny.

"Where's my hot soup?" Danny cried. "Can't anyone get any freakin' service around here?"

Robin couldn't stand it any longer. "Danny!"

"What, babe?"

She rose to her feet, glaring at him with angry eyes. "We're leaving right now."

"Huh?"

She grabbed his arm. "Come on, I'm taking you out of here."

Danny's face tightened into a scowl. His eyelids drooped and his lip curled. Robin had never seen this kind of anger from Danny. It was frightening.

"Danny—"

He stood up quickly, knocking over his chair. "You think you're so cool!"

Now they were all staring at Robin and her date. Someone left the room to call for a security guard. Skip was also out of his chair, standing behind Robin.

Robin touched Danny's shoulder. "Please, don't do this—"

Danny pushed her hand away. "Don't touch me, you freakin' hypocrite. You think you're so much better than me."

"No, Danny," Robin said, "you're just—"

"Shut up!" he cried. "All of you, shut your freakin' mouths. You're not better'n me. You hear that? I'm as good as all of you! I'm

better, 'cause I don't look down my nose at
people from Pitney Docks. To hell with all of
you."

Skip stepped around Robin, reaching for
Danny. "Okay, Kovack, you've shown your
true colors. Time for you to leave." He
grabbed Danny's shoulder.

But Danny wasn't going peacefully. He
swung a hard right hand, catching Skip in
the jaw. Gasps were heard around the room
as Skip slumped to the floor, out cold.

"No!" Robin cried, putting her hands over
her face.

Someone else tried to subdue Danny. Another punch sent a waiter tumbling into a
serving cart. The guests began to rise from
their tables, anticipating trouble as Robin's
boyfriend went berserk.

"I hate all of you!" Danny cried. "All of you!"
He tore off his jacket and then ripped the
shirt from his body. Bare-chested, he leapt
onto the table and started kicking the plates
and napkins. His foot launched the floral
centerpiece into the air. The flying centerpiece struck Mrs. Cutshawl in the head,
causing her to faint.

"You're the creeps, not me!" Danny cried.
"Screw all of you. Freakin' snobs!"

Robin drew back against the wall, watching in horror.

Three waiters rushed at Danny, but he was

too quick for them. He kicked one in the head and then jumped from the table, running headlong into the crowd. He punched at anyone who came near him. In his rage, he cleared the dinner tables with one sweeping motion of his arm. Food and drink flew everywhere. Plates and glasses crashed on the floor.

Danny kept railing at the guests, calling them indecent names, swatting at them with his fists. What had set him off? Why was he acting like an animal?

Dr. Anderson appeared at his daughter's side. "Robin, come on, let me get you out of here."

But she could not move. She was frozen against the wall, paralyzed, unable to speak. It had to be a nightmare. She'd wake up in her bed at home.

Only it wasn't a bad dream. Danny had really lost it. And Skip lay on the floor, bleeding from the mouth.

Dr. Anderson caught sight of Skip. "My God!"

He bent to help the fallen boy.

Robin's eyes were fixed on Danny and his destruction.

A group of waiters rushed at Danny. The wild boy leapt onto another table. When the waiters tried to knock the table over, Danny jumped to the next table, using it like a platform. His feet kicked the plates and glasses into the air.

"You losers!" he cried. "Freakin' losers!"

He jumped from table to table until the waiters finally tackled him. They managed to surround Danny, grabbing him, trying to subdue him. But he was too strong, possessed of an unnatural power. He fought off the three waiters and ran loose again, terrorizing the few guests who had not fled.

Tears streaked down Robin's face. Why was he doing this to her? She had been so kind, so generous with Danny. Robin didn't deserve to be humiliated like this. He was ruining the entire Valentine's Day Dance.

The uniformed security guard appeared through the door, holding a nightstick in his hand. He also wore a gun on his hip. Would he have to use the pistol on Danny?

Danny motioned to the guard. "Come on, dude. You and me. Let's mix it up. I'll shove that stick in your ear!"

The guard lunged with the nightstick, trying to hit Danny. Danny dodged the blow and grabbed the stick, wresting it away from the guard. The guard immediately pulled the gun from the holster.

"Don't move another step," the guard told him. "If you—"

Danny swung the nightstick, hitting the guard's wrist. The pistol flew from his hand, landing on the other side of the room. Danny jumped the guard, holding the nightstick against his throat, trying to strangle him.

"I hate cops!" Danny cried. "I hate you all!"

Robin saw someone creeping up behind Danny. A party guest swung a bottle of champagne, smashing Danny in the back of the head. Danny lurched with the blow, but he did not go down. He released the guard and turned toward his attacker. Another bottle bounced off Danny's forehead, thrown by a waiter. The projectile didn't even faze Danny, though it did open up a gash on his forehead.

Blood poured down Danny's face, streaking crimson on his shoulders and his chest. "You can't hurt me!" he cried. "I'm better'n all of you!"

He still held the guard's nightstick in hand. Wielding the club, Danny ran around the room, smashing everything in his path. Broken glass flew in splinters, plates cracked into pieces and the silverware was mangled with each blow.

Where had his rage come from? Why was he out of control? What had set him off?

"Freakin' losers!"

More breaking glass.

The club took out a window.

Glass flew into the air.

Danny drew closer to Robin, cutting a path of destruction along the way. When he finally reached her, he stood there with the night-stick in his hand. His bloody chest heaved and his face no longer resembled the boy she had fallen in love with. This creature was a monster, a demon from the underworld.

Robin's lips parted to form a single, whispered word. "Why?"

But Danny did not reply. Instead, he drew back the club like he was going to hit her. Dr. Anderson rushed suddenly from the side, butting into Danny, knocking him to the ground.

Danny jumped to his feet, growling. "Freakin' losers!"

Dr. Anderson stood in front of his daughter. "Leave her alone, Danny. You've hurt her enough for one evening."

For a lifetime! Robin thought.

A whooping, savage war cry escaped from Danny's guts. He bolted away from the father and daughter, wreaking havoc with the nightstick. The room had cleared so there wasn't anyone for him to hurt now. The security guard, Skip and a couple of waiters lay unconscious on the floor.

"I hope someone called the police," Dr. Anderson muttered.

"No!" Robin said. "He hates the police. They'll just—"

Her father glared at her. "I don't care,

Robin. Do you see what he's done? Isn't this enough for you? Isn't it—"

Robin fled from her father, sobbing. She had to get to Danny again. She had to help him.

But Danny was too far gone. He used the nightstick to break another window. When he had cleared the casement of glass, Danny jumped out into the freezing winter night, rushing around on the grounds of the country club.

Robin stepped to the window, following his movements. Didn't he feel the cold on his bare skin? How could he act so savagely? His behavior had changed in an instant.

"Damn you!" Danny railed to the night. "Damn you all!"

He started to use the nightstick on the tiny lights that illuminated the grounds. Sparks flew each time he smashed a row of the white bulbs. Danny laughed maniacally, as if a devil had entered his body.

Robin heard the sirens moaning over Port City. Pulsating blue lights sped through the entrance of the country club. It didn't take the police long to find Danny. He turned to challenge them with the nightstick.

"Come on, you pigs!" Danny cried. "Arrest this!"

"He's on something," one of the officers said. "Get the Taser!"

For a moment Robin thought they were going to shoot Danny. But instead the police used a stun weapon that was powered by an electrical charge. When Danny rushed at them, they fired the prongs of the weapon into his chest.

Danny stopped dead in the snow. His body began to convulse violently. Robin had to turn away before Danny fell to the ground, twitching and shrieking until he passed out.

"He's finished," one of the officers shouted.

Robin looked back to see the red light of an ambulance. The emergency vehicle pulled in behind the police cruisers. Two paramedics lifted Danny from the ground.

Robin thought she heard the words "angel dust" from the mouth of the emergency technician.

Had Danny taken drugs?

Was that why he had freaked out?

Robin watched as they put Danny's lifeless body into the back of the ambulance. The doors were closed and the vehicle sped away. Her boyfriend was taken from her on what had to be the most awful night of her life.

She and Danny were finished that quickly.

But it wasn't completely over.

Not by a long shot.

ELEVEN

The backseat of the town car was cold and lonely on the ride home from the country club. Snow had begun to fall again, punctuating the bleakness of the horrible evening. Robin sat with her arms folded, staring out the window. She felt numb inside, still gripped by the trauma of watching Danny behave like an animal. She could hear his cries as he wrecked the Valentine's Day Dance.

Dr. Anderson steered the town car toward Prescott Estates without so much as a word to his daughter. Her mother sat on the passenger side, glancing into the rearview mirror to look at Robin. They would hate her forever, Robin thought. They would never forgive her for what had happened.

Robin at least wanted to offer an apology. "Mom, Dad. I—I'm sorry. I—"

Dr. Anderson glared into the rearview mirror, his eyes wide and angry. "We've never told you who to date, Robin, but this boy was a big mistake. Do you understand that?"

Robin nodded. "Yes, sir."

"Why didn't you stay with Skip?" her mother asked.

Robin looked out at the snow. "I don't know. He was boring. He just didn't—"

"Boring!" her father railed. "So what do you call this boy? He wrecked everything tonight. Are you happy, Robin? He could've killed someone. Is that exciting enough for you?"

Tears welled in her eyes. "I said I was sorry!"

"Well, sorry doesn't get it!" Dr. Anderson replied.

She began to sob with her face in her hands. "I didn't mean for this to happen."

"You've got to think, Robin! Do you understand me! You can't just react without some thought behind it!"

Mrs. Anderson looked at her husband. "That's enough for tonight. She's not responsible for the way that boy acted."

But Dr. Anderson wasn't ready to give up his lecture. "Robin, we've taught you to be tolerant of everyone. But that doesn't mean you have to go out with boys like Danny."

"All right!" Robin screamed. "I'll never go out with anyone again! Will that make you happy?"

"Robin—"

"Just shut up!" she told him. "Just leave me alone!"

"That's no way to talk to me!" Dr. Anderson insisted. "You can consider yourself grounded for the next month, young lady."

"Fine!" Robin cried, tears flowing down her cheeks. "You can go to hell for all I care."

"Is that what you learned from Danny? Huh? Is that what he taught you to—"

"Stop it!" Mrs. Anderson said. "Both of you."

Dr. Anderson wanted to protest but when he saw his wife's irate expression, he slumped behind the wheel of the town car.

Robin sobbed in the backseat, wishing that she were dead. It had been the worst night of her life. And it wasn't over yet.

When they reached the house in Prescott Estates, Robin climbed out of the backseat and ran into the house, scaling the stairs to her room. She slammed the door, locking it behind her. She didn't want to talk to her parents anymore. She didn't want to talk to anyone. Robin needed to be alone with her misery.

As she undressed, she threw the evening gown on the floor. It didn't mean anything to her. Not after Danny's little show at the country club. She put on an oversize T-shirt and slid under the sheets of her bed.

Robin closed her eyes but the images would not go away. She was back in the country club. Danny was running amok, fighting everyone, making a fool of himself and her family.

What had gotten into him? One moment he was the perfect gentleman, kissing up to Mrs. Cutshawl. The next minute he was swinging from the rafters, acting like a rabid ape. Had it all simply become too much for him to handle? Or was he on drugs, as someone had suggested?

Robin hadn't seen him take any drugs. Yet, there had been a glassy look in his eyes. She had never seen that look before. And in their private conversations, Danny had confessed that he had been with a bad crowd a couple of years ago, but now Danny shunned the use of drugs and alcohol. She remembered how sad he had seemed when he described the effects of his father's drinking.

So what had happened to set him off?

The phone rang next to her bed, almost sending Robin through the roof. Who would be calling her? Danny?

Reluctantly, she picked up the receiver. "Hello?"

"Robin, this is Skip."

She sighed. Skip was the last person she wanted to talk to on this dreadful night. Robin felt badly about Danny decking Skip and knocking him unconscious. It was all so embarrassing.

"How are you doing?" Robin asked. "Are you okay?"

"I'm fine," Skip replied. "Kovack got in a sucker punch, otherwise I would've floored him."

"I don't really want to talk about this," Robin said.

"I understand, babe. Listen, is there anything I can do for you? I mean, I could come over if you don't want to be alone at a time like this."

"That's all right, Skip. I want to be alone. It's been a rotten day. I just want to go to sleep."

If I can go to sleep, she thought.

Skip exhaled, like he was disappointed. "I understand. Wow, how about that Kovack? What a jerk? Why did he do it, Robin? Why did he act like that?"

"I don't know, Skip."

"Well, look, Robin, I'll check in with you tomorrow. Maybe we can get together. There are a few things I'd like to discuss with you. Okay?"

"Whatever. Good-bye, Skip."

"I'm sorry everything happened, Robin, but maybe it will all work out for the best."

Robin hung up on him. She closed her eyes, hugging the pillow, trying to go to sleep. But the images were still there, plaguing her, refusing to let her drift away.

Danny's voice was haunting, the police sirens screeched in her ears. She heard breaking glass, saw Skip fall to the floor when Danny punched him. Why had it all happened that way?

Maybe it would seem different in the morning.

Maybe the light of day could free her from the nightmare.

But after a fitful, sleepless night, the morning wouldn't be any easier.

A sharp rapping on her door stirred Robin from the darkness. She opened her eyes, feeling worse than she had the night before. Her father called to her, telling her to come downstairs.

"Hurry," he urged. "We have a lot of talking to do."

"Great," Robin muttered to herself.

What now?

Was she going to jail for bringing Danny to the dance?

Robin delayed as long as she could, lingering in the shower and then taking a while to get dressed. But she could not put off the inevitable meeting with her parents. She had to face them.

Dr. Anderson sat at the counter in the kitchen. He looked up when his daughter walked into the brightly lit room. He wasn't smiling this morning. Outside, the snow had stopped but it was still a gloomy day in Port City, overcast and cold with more snow on the way.

Mrs. Anderson stood at the stove, fixing scrambled eggs and toast. She glanced at Robin, trying to offer a smile. But they were tense. Like Robin, they had probably tossed and turned all night.

"Sit down," her father demanded.

Robin pulled up a stool, sitting at the counter. "Hi. I'm sorry about the way I talked to you last night."

Dr. Anderson sighed. "Thank you, Robin. I accept your apology but we have a lot of other things to discuss."

She nodded. "I understand."

"First," Dr. Anderson started, "there's the matter of the damages at the country club. I talked to Mrs. Cutshawl this morning. She says that Danny owes the country club twenty-five hundred dollars for everything that he broke."

"He's lucky that was all," Mrs. Anderson offered as she put a plate of scrambled eggs in front of Robin. "We're all lucky that no one was killed."

"Danny can pay it," Robin said. "He has the money. It'll clean out his college fund, though."

Dr. Anderson grimaced. "Well, he should've thought about that before he ran berserk through the dining room."

"I still can't believe he did that to us," Mrs. Anderson said. "He seemed like such a nice boy."

Robin hesitated, wondering if she should ask the next question. "Uh, do you know what happened to Danny?"

"He's being held at the juvenile detention center in Millbrook," Dr. Anderson replied. "But he's one lucky boy."

"What do you mean?" Robin asked.

Dr. Anderson scowled at her. "Well, I think they ought to throw the book at the little creep, but Mrs. Cutshawl doesn't want to press charges as long as Danny pays for the damages. And she doesn't want any of this in the papers, so we're doing our best to keep it quiet."

Robin sighed and hung her head. "Oh."

"I offered to resign from the country club," her father went on, "but Mrs. Cutshawl won't hear of it. She's being very gracious about this. Luckily for all of us, she doesn't want to make a fuss about everything. You're very fortunate, Robin."

Fortunate? No way, she thought. It would be all over school. Everyone would be talking about the way Robin's boyfriend spoiled the Valentine's Dance at the country club. She'd be the laughingstock of Central Academy.

"And another thing," Dr. Anderson persisted, "you're not to go near that boy, do you understand? Danny Kovack is off-limits to you, Robin. I don't even want you talking to him. Don't look at him, don't encourage him. As long as you're under this roof, you're not to see Danny Kovack again. Is that clear? Robin, look at me."

She glanced up, meeting her father's angry stare. "I understand, Dad. I won't see him."

"Good. Now, another thing—"

The doorbell rang, interrupting the discussion.

"I'll get it," Mrs. Anderson said.

"She left the kitchen to answer the front door.

Dr. Anderson shook a finger at his daughter. "I hope you've learned a valuable lesson here, Robin. If you—"

"Well, look who's here," Mrs. Anderson said, leading Skip into the kitchen. "Skip dropped by to see you, Robin."

Robin grimaced. What was *he* doing here?

She didn't want to see Skip or anyone else for that matter.

Skip smiled bashfully. "Hi, Robin. I thought I'd see how you're doing."

"Fine," Robin said curtly. "How's Candy?"

Skip blushed. "Uh, she's okay."

Dr. Anderson nodded and grinned. "Skipper, I hope that ruckus last night didn't upset you too much. How's the jaw?"

Skip touched his chin. "Okay. Kovack sucker-punched me."

"Well, we should all put last night behind us," Mrs. Anderson offered. "Skip, have you eaten breakfast? Would you like some scrambled eggs and toast?"

"No thank you, Mrs. Anderson. Uh, I was just wondering if Robin wanted to go skiing today. I'm riding up to Cranmore. The snow is supposed to be perfect."

Robin shook her head. "Sorry, Skip. I'm grounded. I can't go anywhere."

"Uh, not so fast," Dr. Anderson chimed in. "I was a little angry last night when I said that. If you want to go skiing with Skip, then I don't see why you shouldn't ride up to Cranmore with him. It sounds like fun."

Mrs. Anderson was also agreeable. "Yes, maybe a day of skiing would be therapeutic after last night."

Skip glanced at Robin with the same old expectant expression that had led her to break up with him in the first place. "What-taya say, Robin? You and me on the slopes?"

Robin shook her head. "No thanks."

"But your parents said it's okay. I—"

"What about Candy?" Robin challenged. "Is she going?"

Skip looked away, embarrassed. "No, she's busy today. Like I said, it would just be you and me."

Robin shook her head. "No thanks, Skip."

"But, honey," her father started. "Skip is—"

"I'm not going!" Robin replied. "And you can't make me."

She ran out of the kitchen, hurrying up the stairs to her room. Robin fell on her bed, sobbing again. She wondered if her parents had encouraged Skip to come by to see her. Was Skip the kind of boy they wanted her to date? They couldn't control her life. They couldn't choose her friends, tell her what to do.

The phone rang, distracting her from the grief. "Hello?"

No voice from the other end.

"Who is this?"

She heard breathing.

"This isn't funny. Who—"

"Robin, it's me, Danny."

Her heart jumped into her throat. For a moment she was angry. Then her concerns rose to the surface. Despite what he had done at the country club, part of her still cared about Danny.

"Where are you?" she asked.

"At Millbrook. Listen, I only get one phone call. Can you call a lawyer for me?"

"You won't need one," Robin replied. "They're not pressing charges. Mrs. Cutshawl says you have to pay for the damages."

"How much?"

"Twenty-five hundred dollars."

Danny sighed. "Bummer, there goes my college money."

"Danny, what happened? Why did you act like that?"

"Robin, I don't remember very much about last night. I know I got into a fight, but—"

Her anger and humiliation swelled again. "A fight? Danny, you trashed the place. You hurt Skip, you broke a window. You were out of control. How could you forget?"

"I don't know, Robin. I—I'm sorry. Maybe if you told me what I did it will all come back to me."

"Forget it, Danny. You're a loser. I can't see you anymore. Just stay away from me."

"Wait, Robin, give me another chance. If you—"

"Good-bye, Danny."

She slammed the phone down and unplugged it.

Robin fell on her pillow, crying again.

Why had everything happened to *her*?

And why did she still care about Danny after what he had done to her and her family?

There was no excuse for his behavior.

She'd just have to forget him.

But he would be hard to avoid.

Danny Kovack would not go away easily.

TWELVE

Monday morning came too quickly for Robin. She had to return to Central Academy after the humiliation of the Valentine's Day disaster at the country club. The sky was bright and the air brisk as she approached the school. In the senior parking lot, she saw a couple of kids who whispered and laughed when they caught sight of the tall, blond-haired girl.

Robin knew she had to forget about everything, to hold her chin high as she walked in the narrow corridor. Had the hall always been this congested? Or did the staring eyes and nasty comments make it seem claustrophobic?

"Hey, Robin, enjoy the dance?"

"Is that her?"

"Yeah, she took the wild man to the country club dance."

"The one who went ballistic?"

"Yeah."

"Cool."

As she approached her locker, Robin saw Paige standing there, waiting for her. Paige tried to smile sympathetically. Robin spun the dial of her combination lock, staring at the wall.

"Did you hear?" Robin asked.

Paige nodded. "Yeah."

"Well, did you come to tell me I was wrong for going out with Danny?" She turned to glare at her best friend. "Huh, Paige?"

Paige shook her head. "No, I came to see if you needed anyone to talk to."

Robin's eyes began to glisten with tears. "Paige, it was awful. Just awful."

Paige gave Robin a hug. "I'm sorry."

Robin drew back, wiping her eyes. "Danny called me from jail. It was terrible."

"What happened?"

Robin shrugged. "I don't know. He just lost it. Paige, I can't believe he'd do that to me."

"You should've called me this weekend," Paige offered.

"I didn't want to talk to anyone."

"I can't blame you," Paige replied.

Robin looked away. "Have you seen Danny today?"

"No. Robin, you'd better stay away from him. I mean, he did it once—"

Paige was interrupted by Candy's arrival. Candy gave Robin a catty, disapproving look. Robin braced herself for the barrage.

"Thanks for ruining the Valentine's Dance," Candy said in a nasty tone. "Why don't you bring Danny next year and see if he can trash that one too?"

Robin hung her head. "I'm sorry, Candy."

"Sorry sucks," Candy went on. "Just stay away from me, Robin. And stay away from Skip while you're at it."

Robin's brow fretted. "Skip?"

"Yes, he's mine," Candy gibed. "You can't have him back just because Danny blew it."

Robin's shame turned to anger. "I don't want Skip back, Candy. Even though he came to my house on Saturday to ask me to go skiing."

Candy's haughtiness disappeared. "What?" Her face contracted into a doeful expression.

"Leave her alone, Candy," Paige said, stepping in to defend Robin. "She feels bad enough."

Candy's lower lip began to tremble. "Just stay away from Skip! I mean it."

"Don't worry, I plan to," Robin replied.

Candy scuttered off down the hall.

Paige wheeled back to Robin. "Did Skip really ask you to go skiing?"

"Yes. But I turned him down."

"Wow, I bet he's still hung up on you. I mean, look at Candy's reaction. She's really jealous."

Robin slammed her locker door. "I don't care about Skip and Candy. They aren't my problem."

Paige sighed. "So, what's going to happen to Danny?"

Robin shrugged and started down the hallway. "He's getting off with just paying the damages."

"Wow. He could've gone to jail."

Robin grimaced, stopping in front of her homeroom. "I don't know, Paige. Everything happened so quickly."

"What do you mean?"

"Danny just lost it all of a sudden. For no reason."

"I heard he was on drugs," Paige said.

"I didn't see him take them."

The bell rang, calling them to class.

"I hope Danny doesn't cause any trouble for you, Robin."

Robin took a deep breath. "Neither do I, Paige. Neither do I."

All day, Robin watched for Danny, but he never presented himself. She expected him to be there in English class, but his desk was empty. He had ditched school, no doubt to avoid the humiliation that Robin had experienced.

When the final bell rang, Robin hurried to her locker, opening it quickly. Something fluttered to the floor. She picked up a piece of heavy bonded drawing paper. A crudely drawn heart had been colored with red crayon. A long, jagged knife pierced the heart and the words "Be My Valentine" had been scrawled under the heart.

"Danny," Robin whispered.

Someone touched her shoulder. She glanced up to see him standing there. Danny Kovack stared at her with a dull gleam in his dark eyes.

Robin stepped back. "Danny—"

"I blew off school today, but I just had to see you. Robin, you have to tell me what happened. I don't remember very much."

She shook her head slowly. "Danny, I can't see you anymore. We've broken up. After the way you acted—"

"How did I act?" Danny asked frantically. "I mean, everyone keeps telling me that I was out of control. And I had to pay damages, almost everything I have in the bank. My college fund is gone."

Robin felt the anger swelling inside her. She was face-to-face with him, the demon who had trashed the country club, the devil who had ruined the Valentine's Dance. There were so many things she wanted to say to him. But she never got the chance.

"Kovack! Get away from her!"

Skip's voice boomed down the hallway. He stormed toward Danny and Robin with three of his friends flanking him. Danny wheeled to face them. There was going to be a fight. But this time, Robin didn't care. After what he had done at the dance, Danny deserved whatever they gave him.

Skip stood in front of Danny, challenging him. "Want to throw a sucker punch now, Kovack?"

Danny grimaced. "I hit you?"

"You hit a lot of people, Kovack. You should be proud of yourself for showing everyone what you're really all about."

Danny held up his hands. "Whoa, I don't want any trouble, Skip. I mean—"

"Trouble?" Skip guffawed. "You can't avoid trouble, Kovack. That's why you're going to stay away from Robin. Can you understand me or do we have to show you?"

"Three against one," Danny said, looking back at Robin.

Robin hung her head. "Just go, Danny. Please."

Danny began to quiver. "Robin—"

"You heard her, Kovack," Skip said. "Clear out."

Danny looked back and forth between

them. "You're back with the hockey-head, aren't you, Robin?"

Robin stiffened, steeling herself against the tide of conflicting emotions that surged inside her. She knew she could not keep seeing Danny. But she still had feelings for him. It broke her heart. Danny seemed so hopeless, so desperate. Would he lose control again? She couldn't take the chance.

"I still love you, Robin," Danny offered.

She shook her head. "No, it won't work, Danny. I broke up with you. Live with it."

"Accept it," Skip blurted out.

Danny scowled at them, reminding Robin of the face she had seen at the country club debacle. "I shoulda known better than to get mixed up with you Prescott types. So long, Robin. You and hockey-boy can have each other."

Danny stomped off, leaving Robin and Skip together.

Skip smiled at Robin. "Don't worry, I'm not going to let him hurt you."

Robin sighed. "Thanks."

"Let me walk you to your car," Skip offered.

Robin really didn't want to hang out with Skip and his friends. But Danny might try to come after her again. And she didn't want to be alone with Danny. He was too dangerous.

"All right," Robin said.

Skip turned to his friends. "I'll meet you guys later."

When they were gone, he started toward the senior parking lot, staying close to Robin. Outside in the frigid air, Robin listened for the sound of a motorcycle. But there was too much snow for Danny to be riding his bike.

"I can't believe the nerve of that guy," Skip said. "Robin, would you like me to come home with you to—"

"I don't think that will be necessary," Robin replied quickly. "I mean, Candy is mad at me, Skip. She doesn't want me to hang around with you."

Skip sighed and shook his head. "She's too hung up on me, Robin. All that stuff about going steady—I never asked Candy to go with me. But when she started it, I didn't have the heart to—"

Robin held up her palm. "I don't want to know about you and Candy, Skip. That's none of my business."

Skip stopped her, putting his hands on her shoulders, spinning her toward him. "Robin, I care about you. We're friends, okay? If you need anything, just call me. Especially if you have any more trouble with that creep Kovack."

"Just *friends*, though," Robin told him. "We aren't getting back together, Skip."

"Hey, I know that. See ya, Robin."

He opened the car door.

Robin drove off, turning onto Rockbury Lane, heading for Middle Road. On the way, she passed Danny who was walking toward Pitney Docks. He waved and called to her, but Robin just kept going. She had to forget about Danny. He wasn't right for her.

Would anyone ever come along who *was* right for her?

When Robin was home alone in her room, she threw her books on the bed. The strange heart drawing fell out of her papers. She looked at the heart with the knife through it. Who would do something like this? Was Danny really capable of such sickness?

Yes, she thought, *I've seen him in action.*

The phone rang, making her heart skip a beat.

"Hello?"

She heart heavy breathing.

"Who is this?" Robin demanded.

"It's not over," a voice said.

"Who is this?"

Click!

Robin hung up. The voice had sounded male, though she was sure the caller had been trying to disguise it. *Danny.*

It's not over.

Danny.

Who else could it be?

The phone rang again. Reluctantly, Robin

picked up the receiver. She was going to give the person on the other end a piece of her mind. But it wasn't Danny.

"Robin, this is Candy. I'm warning you. Stay away from Skip or I'll scratch your eyes out."

"Candy, Skip and I are just friends. We—"

Click!

Robin sighed deeply, wondering if things could get any worse.

THIRTEEN

After a sleepless night, Robin went down to breakfast looking tired and worn. Her parents noticed that she was depressed, but they didn't say anything. Robin chose not to tell them about the weird message in her locker. Nor did she mention the phone calls. She figured they would blame her for going out with Danny Kovack in the first place. After all, hadn't her relationship with Danny started everything? Now that they had broken up, Robin would just have to ride it out. Everything would be smoothed over sooner or later. Sooner, Robin hoped.

She ate breakfast and said good-bye to her mother and father. The drive to school was lonely. It was another cold day, threatening snow. Robin had to wonder if Danny would try to approach her again. Would he be in school today?

As she parked her car, she kept looking for him. Would he try to hurt her? She couldn't forget how violent he had been at the country club dance.

Robin entered the senior classroom building, glancing all around her, expecting Danny to appear at any moment. Maybe she should go to the assistant principal, tell him about Danny. The eerie phone call still rang in her ears.

It's not over.

What did Danny have planned for her?

As she spun the combination lock, she braced herself for any notes that might fall out of her locker. But there was nothing on this winter morning. Robin found the books she needed and then closed the locker door, turning away to bump into a tall boy.

She startled, falling back, expecting Danny to be all over her. "No, please—"

Skip touched her shoulders. "Hey, take it easy. It's just me. I was going to walk you to homeroom."

Robin started to reply, but then she caught a glimpse of Candy who was watching them from down the hallway. Candy's narrow eyes glared at Robin. Did Skip have any idea that Candy was so jealous?

"How are you doing?" Skip asked. "Is Danny bothering you?"

Robin shook her head. "No, I'm fine, Skip. I

have to get to homeroom. Excuse me." She pushed past him, walking toward Candy.

Candy scowled as Robin passed her. "Slut!"

Robin ignored her, hurrying to her homeroom.

The remainder of the morning was like a dull waking dream. Robin went through the motions, barely paying attention in her classes. She managed to avoid running into Danny, though she did see him a couple of times in the hall. He was in school, so she would have to see him in English class.

Sure enough, when she walked into the classroom, Danny sat at his desk, gazing at her with a longing expression. Everyone seemed to snicker and whisper. Robin plopped down in the desk, feeling the stares on her back.

Mrs. Traxler glared at Robin but then she began class as if nothing were wrong. Halfway through the lecture, a note dropped on Robin's desk, passed across the aisles by Danny.

Robin froze, wondering if the note was another threat.

It's not over.

She glanced sideways, looking at him. Danny nodded to her, urging Robin to read the note. She unfolded the paper, scanning the bold printing.

I'm sorry about everything. Please forgive me. I have to talk to you. It's important.

Robin wadded up the note, dropping it on the floor. She did not look at Danny again. When the bell rang, she hurried from the classroom to get away from him.

What could he possibly have to say to her? In spite of Danny's cryptic message, it *was* over. They had broken up and she wasn't going to see him anymore.

Robin returned to her locker, holding her breath in anticipation of another note. Nothing there, except books and notebooks. Maybe Danny would give up when he realized that she did not want to have anything to do with him.

"Robin—"

She turned to see Danny standing there. "Get away from me," she told him. "I don't want to talk to you."

"Robin, you have to listen to me. I think I figured out what happened that night at the country club. It wasn't my fault—"

Her expression became angry, hate-filled. "Whose fault was it then, Danny? Huh? You were the one who trashed the place. You ruined my life."

He grabbed her shoulders. "Robin, please, listen to me—"

She tried to turn away.

Danny wouldn't let go. "Robin, you have to listen!"

"No, I don't. Danny—"

Suddenly he released his grip on her. Danny flew backward, crashing against the lockers. When he tried to move toward her, Skip and his friends restrained Danny.

"You just don't give up, do you, Kovack?" Skip said.

"To hell with you," Danny replied. "You'd better get off me, Chesterton."

Skip put a finger in Danny's face. "You don't seem to be catching on, Kovack. Stay away from Robin. You got it?"

"Or what?" Danny challenged. "You and your boys gonna gang up on me?"

"That's right," Skip replied. "We'll make you wish you had never seen us."

Skip pushed Danny away from the lockers.

Danny stumbled a few feet before he gained his balance. He looked back at Robin with pleading eyes. She turned a cold shoulder, ignoring him.

"Robin, I have to talk to you!" Danny cried. "I can explain everything."

Skip and his buddies had formed a shield in front of Robin.

"Get out of here, Kovack," Skip snarled. "And leave Robin alone, if you know what's good for you."

Danny took a step toward them, but he had to retreat in the face of superior numbers.

"What a jerk," Skip said.

Robin drew an uneven breath. "Thanks, Skip."

Skip smiled at her. "Hey, anytime. You want me to come over tonight and hang out with you? I could—"

"That's okay," Robin replied. "I'll be fine. Danny has to give up sooner or later."

Skip nodded. "I understand. Listen, you call me if you need anything."

"Sure."

Robin walked away from them, wondering if Candy had seen Skip coming to her rescue. She didn't want to interfere with their relationship. She had already ruined her own life. Why spread the bad luck to her friends?

The day ended with Robin heading for the gymnasium. She had to dress out and make an effort to work on the weight machine. Soccer practice would begin in a couple of weeks, though Robin could hardly think about sports right now.

As she strode across the plaza, braving the cold wind, she thought she saw someone watching her from the corner of the gym. Her chest tightened and her body tingled. Was Danny stalking her? For a moment she wished Skip were there. But then the shadowy figure darted away, disappearing behind the gym.

That's it," Robin thought. *I'm going to report him. I'll speak to the assistant principal.*

She entered the gym, hurrying back to the locker room. Robin was the first one there. Or so she thought. A shower gushed in one of the stalls, billowing steam into the locker area. The entire room had been steeped in a ghostly vapor.

Robin grimaced. "Who left the darned shower on?"

She waved at the mist, making her way back to the shower stall. Robin threw back the curtain and screamed loudly when she saw the bleeding girl slumped on wet tile. A solid stream of crimson flowed from the slits in the girl's wrists, emptying the last of her crimson life force into a whirling eddy that disappeared down the drain.

The dead girl's bluish face wore a death mask. Her eyes were open, the jaw gaping. A single-edged razor blade lay on the tile near her fingers. For a moment Robin didn't recognize her.

Then the face came into focus.

"Oh my God. Candy!"

Robin covered her face. She couldn't believe that Candy had taken her own life. Robin became weak, light-headed, nauseous. She stood there, paralyzed until a voice in the back of her head told Robin to get help right away.

FOURTEEN

Candy's funeral was held the following Friday on a cold, blustery day that threatened snow again. A large crowd turned out despite the weather. Candy had been a popular girl, well known, an athlete and a good student. No one could believe that she had committed suicide. There had been no warning signs, no telltale indications that Candy had been suffering enough to slash her wrists in the shower of the girls' locker room.

Robin stood between her parents, watching as Candy's coffin was lowered into the cold earth. Ever since finding Candy in the shower, Robin had dreamed about the incident. In one of the many nightmares, Candy had risen from death, pointing a bloody finger at Robin, blaming her for the suicide.

Robin shuddered at the memory of the

dream. Her father put his arm around her. Mrs. Anderson drew closer to comfort her grieving daughter. Robin hadn't been particularly fond of Candy, but she hadn't wanted Candy to die either.

"Ashes to ashes," the pastor recited, "dust to dust. We commend our dear departed sister Candace to the earth so that she may rest in the arms of God our Father, in Jesus' name, Amen."

No one really knew why Candace had taken her own life. The only clue had been a cryptic message scrawled on the shower tile with a black, indelible marker. Five words: *I can't take it anymore.*

What was it that Candy couldn't take? She had been jealous of Robin and Skip, even though there hadn't been any reason for Candy to be jealous. Robin remembered Candy's warning for her to stay away from Skip. Had Candy thought that Robin and Skip were getting back together?

Robin glanced over at Skip who stood with several of his buddies from the hockey team. Tears streaked down Skip's reddened cheeks. His body trembled as he blubbered in grief. He had made some comment about Candy being obsessed with him. Had Skip been the reason that she had slashed her wrists?

I can't take it anymore.

When the coffin hit bottom in the grave,

the crowd started to disperse. Robin lingered for a moment. Her parents told her they'd wait in the car. Robin replied that she'd be along shortly. She just wanted a few minutes to be alone at the gravesite.

As soon as her parents had left, Skip approached her, sobbing. "Robin, I know it was *me*. Candy did it over *me*."

Robin exhaled, shuddering again. "Skip—"

He embraced her, crying on Robin's shoulder. "I cared about Candy," he whimpered. "But she wanted too much, more than I could give her, Robin."

Robin patted his back. "It's all right, Skip. No one knew that she was so—so disturbed."

Skip drew back, wiping his eyes. "I never had a clue, Robin. Nothing, not one sign. If I had known—" He broke down again, crying and shaking.

"It's going to be all right," Robin told him, though her tone was blank. "It's not your fault."

"But I could've done something, Robin!"

"If we had known, any one of us could've done something, Skip. But we didn't know. Don't torture yourself."

A faint smile spread over Skip's thin mouth. "I knew I could count on you, Robin. Listen, I don't want to be alone at a time like this. Why don't we go get something to eat?"

Robin shook her head. "I'm sorry, Skip, I'm

going home. I just want to be alone. Why
don't you go with your friends?" She nodded
toward the members of the hockey team who
waited for Skip.

He sighed. "Sure. Listen, would you mind if
I called you later? Just to talk?"

Robin smiled a little. "No problem. Good-
bye, Skip."

She turned to walk away from the grave.
As she approached her father's car, Robin
caught sight of a familiar figure standing on
the other side of Middle Road. She stopped
and stared at Danny Kovack who leaned
against Doreen's old car, a beat-up Ford Fairmont that was a faded shade of navy-blue.
Doreen wasn't with him, but they were probably back together if she had let him use the
car.

Another shiver invaded Robin's body. What
was Danny doing here? He hadn't been
friends with Candy. And Candy had despised
Danny for what he had done to ruin the
Valentine's Dance. There was no reason for
Danny to be at the funeral.

Danny took a step away from the car. For a
moment Robin thought he was going to come
after her. But then he wheeled around suddenly, climbing into the blue Fairmont, chug-
ging off down the street with black exhaust
streaming from the tailpipe.

Robin took a deep breath. She had figured

it was over with Danny. Did Danny have plans to come after her? She hurried to her father's town car, jumping into the backseat.

"Let's go home," she said. "And hurry."

Dr. Anderson turned around, looking at her. "Was that Danny Kovack in the blue car?"

Robin nodded. "Yes."

Her father's face turned bright red. "I'm going to the police. That little punk will leave you alone once and for all."

"No, Dad!" Robin cried. "Please!"

"Robin, if he bothers you—"

"He hasn't been bothering me, Dad. It's okay. You don't have to go to the police."

Dr. Anderson sighed. "All right. But if he bothers you again, I'm talking to Chief Danridge."

He put the car into gear and rolled home toward Prescott Estates.

Robin glanced out the window, peering at the snow-covered landscape. She had talked to the police chief, Victor Danridge, during the investigation of Candy's suicide. Robin hadn't been much help. But then again, nobody had the answer to Candy's death. Maybe she had killed herself over Skip, but no one would ever know exactly why she had done it.

As soon as they arrived at the house in Prescott Estates, Robin went straight to her room and locked the door. Classes at Central had been canceled for the day. She almost wished that school were on, as it would give her something to do besides feel sad and lonely.

The phone rang, chilling her bones. "Hello?"

"Hi, it's me, Paige."

"Oh. Hi. I didn't see you at the funeral."

"I was in the back," Paige replied. "I was also one of the first people to leave. How are you doing?"

Robin fell on her bed, sighing. "Not too great."

"Listen," Paige went on, "are you busy this weekend?"

"No, just me and my depression," Robin replied. "What'd you have in mind?"

"Nothing much. It's just, well, my father said we could have the cabin up at Thunder Lake if we wanted to get away."

Robin sat up on her bed. "Thunder Lake?"

"Yeah. We could hang out, go cross-country skiing, maybe do some ice skating on the lake. It's still frozen this time of year. What do you think?"

"I'm there," Robin replied. "Let me clear it with Mom and Dad. Call me back in ten, okay?"

A getaway weekend was just what Robin needed. Blow off Port City, try to put everything behind her, get some perspective on the events of the past few months. She had been to the cabin at Thunder Lake many times before. It would do her some good to leave town for a couple of days.

Her mother and father were agreeable to the idea. They gave her fifty dollars and told her to take plenty of warm clothes. Robin returned to her room to begin packing.

Then the phone rang. "Hello?"

Heavy breathing, followed by "It's not over, Robin!"

"To hell with you, Danny Kovack!"

She hung up, trembling.

Again the phone rang. Robin didn't want to pick up. But it might be Paige, calling her back.

"Hello?"

"Hi, Robin, it's me, Skip."

She hesitated. "Oh."

"I just wanted to talk to you—"

"Uh, Skip, I'm going away for the weekend, so I'm really busy with packing."

"Where are you going?" he asked.

"Up to Thunder Lake, at the cabin, you know, Paige's father has a place up there."

Skip exhaled dejectedly. "Oh. Hey, can I come along? I'm really down, Robin. I—"

"Uh, I don't think so, Skip. Look, I don't mean to be short, but I have to go. I'll see you in school on Monday."

Click.

She hated to brush Skip off. He was depressed and lonely. But she didn't want anyone else along for the weekend. Robin just wanted to relax and try to have a good time.

But it wouldn't happen.

FIFTEEN

Robin's Escort rolled north on the turnpike, heading toward Thunder Lake and the cabin that belonged to Paige's father. Robin had asked Paige to drive. The last-minute phone call from Danny had been unsettling for her. She didn't want to think about him anymore. Robin wasn't sure if it was possible to put the nightmare behind her, but she was ready to try.

Paige glanced over at Robin, smiling. "Hey, are you okay?"

Robin sighed and looked out at the snow-covered landscape. "I think I'm going to make it," she replied. "I wonder if it's going to snow?"

Paige shrugged. "The sky is certainly dark enough. What did the weather forecast say?"

"I didn't hear it. Let's try the radio."

Robin switched on the radio and searched the tuner until she found a clear station. It was almost five o'clock, so they got the weather report at the top of the hour. The call was for flurries but no heavy snow and a low temperature of twelve degrees. Saturday would be sunny with highs in the thirties.

"Looks like we're going to have a pretty good weekend," Paige offered. "We'd better stop before we get to the lake. We need some groceries."

"I have money," Robin offered. "Is there a grocery store on the way?"

"I think at the next exit."

Robin smiled at her best friend. "Thanks for asking me, Paige. I really need a break."

"You've certainly been through the grinder lately," Paige replied. "But I think it's going to be all right now."

"I hope so," Robin said, exhaling.

Paige took the next exit and found the grocery store. They ambled down the aisles, grabbing what they needed for the weekend. Robin was starting to relax, even though she could still hear the threatening words in her head.

It's not over.

Why couldn't Danny face the fact that they were finished? How long would he be obsessive? And would he do something drastic?

Paige glanced sideways at her. "Are you okay?"

"No, not completely. I wonder if we should've brought Hank along. You know, have a guy around in case—"

"Hank went out of town with his parents," Paige replied.

"At least you have a boyfriend," Robin said. "A nice guy like Hank. He's a sweetheart."

Paige grinned. "I know."

They paid for the groceries and headed out to the parking lot. As they approached the Escort, Robin stopped dead, gaping at the faded blue Fairmont that rested on the other side of the parking lot. It couldn't be! But there he was, sitting behind the wheel, watching them from the distance.

"What is it?" Paige asked.

Robin nodded toward the Fairmont. "Danny Kovack!"

Paige peered at the blue car. "No! Are you sure?"

"I saw the car at the funeral today," Robin replied. "It belongs to Danny's old girlfriend."

Paige grimaced and shook her head. "Damn him. Come on, we'll lose him on the highway. Your car can outrun that wreck."

They loaded the groceries and got into the car. Paige gunned the throttle, roaring through the parking lot. Robin glanced over her shoulder to see the Fairmont pulling out behind them, following the Escort from a distance.

"He's coming after us," Robin said.

Paige glanced into the rearview mirror. The Fairmont followed them onto the entrance ramp for the turnpike. Paige floored the accelerator, speeding up quickly.

"Is he still there?" she asked.

Robin nodded. "Yeah, but he's farther back. The nerve of that idiot."

"Maybe we should find a cop?"

Robin shook her head. "No. Danny can smell a cop a mile away. He'll just hide for a while and then come after us again."

Paige sighed and gripped the steering wheel. "Hold on then. I'll try something."

Robin glanced at the speedometer. Paige was going eighty-five miles an hour. The Escort had never been driven at such a high speed. The tiny car began to shimmy and shake.

"Paige—"

"Hold on, Robin. I'm going to do it at the next exit. If I get lucky—"

"Paige, I don't know—"

Robin glanced back to see that Danny was getting closer.

Paige didn't slow down as she turned onto the next exit ramp. The Escort flew off the turnpike, heading for a spur road. Robin gripped the sides of her seat, wondering what Paige had in mind. Did she know what she was doing?

Robin saw the red stop light ahead. She glanced back again but she didn't see Danny now. Paige kept the car moving toward the traffic light, which was still red.

"Paige—"

"Brace yourself," Paige told her. "This is the place I was thinking of. Now, if the light will just turn green!"

Robin held her breath as the Escort barreled toward the red light. Paige made no effort to slow down. If they blew under the stop signal, they might hit another car in the intersection. At eighty-five miles an hour, death would be instantaneous.

"Paige!"

"It's going to change," Paige cried.

But the light didn't turn green. Paige tore through the empty intersection, pushing her luck to cheat the grim reaper. The Escort shot up the ramp that would take them back onto the turnpike. In the short span of a few seconds, they had left the main highway and then returned.

Robin glanced back to see if the Fairmont was there. "I think we lost him."

Paige looked in the rearview mirror, smiling. "He's probably wondering what happened to us."

Robin wiped the sweat from her forehead. "Geez, Paige, I thought you were going to kill us back there."

"We aren't finished yet, Robin. Danny may figure out what we did. Keep watching."

Robin peered through the rear windshield, expecting to see the Fairmont. But it was no longer there. Had Danny lost the trail at the intersection below the ramp?

"I don't see him."

"We're getting off at the next exit," Paige told her.

"Is that the exit for Thunder Lake?"

"No, but I know a back way to the cabin. Cross your fingers and hope we make it to the next exit before Danny sees us."

Robin watched nervously as a blue car came up behind them. But it wasn't Danny. The car passed the Escort and kept going.

Paige took the next exit, emerging on a narrow rural highway. Robin's eyes were trained on the rear windshield for at least another ten minutes. But there was no sign of Danny.

She turned forward, slumping in the seat. "We lost him."

Paige switched on the headlights. "Great. That was close. He has some nerve following us."

"He doesn't know where the cabin is, so once we get there, we're safe."

Paige breathed a sigh of relief. "I hope so."

Light snow flurries began to fall as they followed the narrow road. After fifteen minutes of driving, Paige turned off the paved highway, following a dark path back into the forest. Luckily, the Escort was front-wheel drive, so they had no trouble reaching the cabin in the trees.

"Home at last," Paige joked.

Robin unhooked her seat belt and opened the door. "Let's unload the groceries."

They carried the bags into the cabin, which was small but cozy. Robin started a fire in the wood stove while Paige switched on the lights. It would take a while before the cabin was warm so they kept their coats on. Robin opened a couple of cans of soup, putting them into a pan that she set on top of the wood stove.

As she stirred the soup, the whining sound of a small engine echoed outside the cabin in the cold air. Robin stiffened, thinking that Danny had arrived on his motorcycle. He had found them in the middle of the wilderness.

Paige saw the terror in Robin's eyes. "Hey, snap out of it! They're only snowmobiles. They ride out here all the time."

Robin exhaled, trembling. "Sorry."

Paige patted her shoulder. "Don't worry, it's going to be fine. Nobody can hurt you out here. Danny will never find us. Okay?"

Robin nodded. "You're right, Paige. You're right."

But Paige couldn't have been more wrong.

SIXTEEN

The sun glistened off the thick, crunchy trail of snow that Robin and Paige followed on cross-country skis. Robin's arms and legs pumped hard, propelling her over the white carpet. They had skied all the way around Thunder Lake. Robin's body tingled from the exercise. She had worked hard all day and she felt great.

Paige skied behind Robin, losing ground as Robin bolted ahead. Paige tried to keep up, but Robin was too fast. Paige knew her best friend had burned off some of the fear and hostility that had plagued Robin's life of late. Maybe the old Robin would come back today.

"Hey," Paige called, "wait up!"

Paige's voice echoed through the trees. Thick forest stretched on both sides of the trail. There had been a few clearings along the way, but for the most part, Thunder Lake was surrounded by the woods. And in her effort to keep up with Robin, Paige inadvertently let the tip of her right ski stray off the path, catching the low-hanging branch of a snow-laden fir tree.

Paige tumbled into the snow, rolling a few times before she came to a halt. Robin had already turned around upon hearing Paige's cry. She watched Paige's flight and hard landing.

Robin dug in, racing back to help Paige. She hoped that her friend hadn't broken anything. Robin wasn't sure how far they were from the cabin. The cabin didn't have a phone either, so Robin would have to take Paige to the nearest hospital if any of her injuries were serious.

Robin slid to a halt and lifted her ski goggles. "Paige, are you all right?"

Paige groaned as she sat up. "They moved the trail on me."

"Where does it hurt?" Robin asked.

"Mainly my body," Paige replied. "But I don't think anything is broken. Help me up."

Robin extended her hand, pulling Paige to her feet. Paige wobbled for a moment but she gradually regained her balance. She was tired, spent. They had put in a tough day of skiing.

"Can you make it?" Robin asked.

Paige nodded. "I think so."

Robin gazed back down the icy path, peering in the direction of the cabin. Shafts of sunlight streaked the trail, flashing through the opening in the trees. It was beautiful. She was glad she had come with Paige to Thunder Lake.

"How are *you* feeling?" Paige asked.

Robin glanced back at her, smiling. "I'm psyched. This was just what I needed. I forgot what exercise can do."

"Good, I was worried about you."

"How far away from the cabin are we?" Robin asked.

Paige turned her head, taking stock of the landmarks around the trail. "We're pretty close," she replied. "If you want to go fast, I'll meet you there."

Robin laughed a little. "Okay, I'll scout ahead. If I get there first, I'll come back and meet you."

"Thanks," Paige said sarcastically. "Don't let me get in the way, Robin. I'm just a dweeb when it comes to skiing."

"I'll go slow if you—"

"No, have fun," Paige said. "Don't mind me."

"Are you sure?"

"Just go, I'll catch up."

Robin smiled. "Thanks."

She turned away from Paige, pushing off

with the ski poles. In a few seconds she returned to the skating motion that propelled her swiftly along the trail. The trail was firm and packed, perfect for skiing.

Robin had to pump harder to get up a slight incline that rose between the trees. As she crested the rise, she saw a vehicle coming at her from the other side of the trail. A snowmobile roared straight for a head-on collision with a petrified cross-country skier.

But Robin's nerves were in tune. Everything connected giving her instant command of her reflexes. She veered to her left, shooting off the trail, landing with her skis pointed straight ahead. Robin slid through the trees, arriving at the frozen edge of Thunder Lake.

She spun back toward the whirring sound of the snowmobile as it disappeared in the shadows of the forest. "You idiot!" she cried, raising her fist.

She shuddered as she turned her skis around. For a moment she moved slowly on the snow, trying to get back to the main trail. What kind of fool drove a snowmobile on a cross-country trail? she wondered. Did he realize how dangerous it was? Snowmobiles were supposed to stick to their established tracks, not to use the paths set aside for skiers.

Skiers!

It hit her like an avalanche. *Paige!* She was

still on the trail. Had the snowmobile—
Paige!

Robin trembled all over but she managed
to ski her way to the top of the rise. "Paige!"

No immediate reply.

"My God," Robin said softly.

A speeding snowmobile could kill a person.
It happened once or twice every winter.
Snowmobiles colliding with an unsuspecting
victim, snowmobiles crashing into trees, going through the ice on a frozen lake.

"Paige!"

Robin turned to ski back toward her friend.
She was afraid of what she might find. After
everything Robin had been through, she
wasn't sure she could live with the loss of
another friend.

"Paige!"

Robin saw the crumpled body lying between the trees. She hovered above the fallen
girl, hoping that Paige was alive. Robin lifted
her goggles, squinting at the motionless form
in the snow.

"Paige!"

A voice rose from the snow. "Don't just
stand there, help me up, Robin."

Robin lifted Paige from the snow and
steadied her on the trail. "Did that snowmobile run you off the path?" she asked.

Paige grimaced. "Snowmobile?"

"Yeah, some clown almost hit me at the top of the trail. He came this way."

"I heard something," Paige replied, "but I didn't see anything. I took a header into the woods so he probably went by me."

Robin peered into the shadows that were forming between the trees. Was that the whine of a motorized vehicle? Danny knew about engines, he could handle a snowmobile.

"What's wrong?" Paige asked.

Robin shook her head, shuddering, her breath fogging the cold air. "Nothing. Come on, let's get to the cabin."

They skied up the trail and over the rise. Robin saw the cabin ahead of them. They made it back safely without another sighting of the snowmobile.

Paige sat on a stump next to the woodpile. "That was great, but I'm glad it's over." She began to remove her skis.

Robin took a deep breath and peered toward the lake. "Wow, look at it."

Shafts of orange sunlight illuminated the frozen surface of Thunder Lake. It was a huge body of icy water. No wonder it had taken them all day to ski around it.

"What's wrong?" Paige asked.

Robin sighed. "I don't know. That snowmobile shook me up. I'm still tense."

Paige shuddered. "There's ice skates in the shed. You like to skate, don't you?"

"I love it."

Paige nodded toward the lake. "Go on. Take it easy, though. This late in the season, there might be some thin spots, especially over the spring holes."

Robin skied toward a small shed, opening the door. A pair of skates hung on the wall. Robin slid down to the edge of Thunder Lake, removing the skis. She had to sit in the snow to put on the skates. After she moved onto the ice, it didn't take Robin long to find her balance.

"I'll get a fire going!" Paige called. "Don't stay too long. I'll be dark in a while. And don't go too far out!"

Robin waved and pushed off on the sharp blades, skirting across the ice. Her arms and legs worked in perfect rhythm. The air whipped by her face as she rushed toward the middle of the lake. This was what she needed. Athletics had always been a part of her life. To hell with Danny! She'd concentrate on soccer again. The season wasn't far off.

Her long blond hair whirled in the breeze as Robin maneuvered on the ice. She skated backward, performed a spinning turn and then tried a leap that sent her sprawling to the ice. Robin landed on her backside, swirling to a stop on the frozen surface.

The pain from the fall wasn't too bad.

Nothing broken. But as she started to stand up, a cracking sound rose from beneath her. The ice was beginning to break. Robin held her breath, crawling on hands and knees. She didn't want to go through the ice. With the heavy skates on her feet, she'd surely sink to her death in the dark, cold waters of Thunder Lake.

She crawled until the cracking noise ceased. Slowly, she stood up on the skates. The ice held beneath her. Robin pushed off, skating back toward the cabin. She went slowly at first, gradually picking up speed, telling herself that the day was going to be over as soon as she got back to the shore. Robin didn't want to tempt fate anymore. A quiet night by the fire would be enough.

As she approached the snow-laced bank at the edge of the lake, Robin heard the faint whine of a snowmobile. The noise died quickly somewhere behind the cabin. Robin slid to a stop, spraying ice shavings into the air. She lifted her eyes to the bright windows of the cabin. Smoke poured from the chimney pipe. She could see shadows as Paige moved around inside.

It was time to hang up the skis and the skates, Robin told herself. She needed to sit down with a cup of hot chocolate and think things over. Had she learned anything from all this? Or had it simply been her fault for going out with Danny in the first place, for thinking she could change him?

She stepped off the ice, her eyes focused on the orange casements of the cabin windows. Paige appeared in the window for a moment. She waved at Robin, who waved back.

But then Paige was gone, jerked away from the casement by someone who had appeared behind her. At first, Robin thought Paige had fallen. But then she saw the shadows against the wall. Paige struggled with an intruder, trying to fight him off.

"No!" Robin cried. "Danny, don't do it!"

She tried to run in the skates. Robin lost her balance, tumbling to the snow. She had to remove the skates before she could walk on the ground. Her fingers fumbled with the laces. One of the strings knotted on her. She had to remove her gloves to untie the lace. All the time, she kept glancing back at the shadows inside the cabin. When the skates were off, Robin stood up, her stockinged feet pressing into the snow.

The shadows had stopped moving inside the cabin.

Robin ran through the snow to get to her friend.

As she neared the front door of the cabin, a snowmobile blasted to life, roaring off into the trees, fleeing the scene. Robin couldn't see the driver's face. He wore a helmet with a dark face shield.

"Paige!"

She pushed into the cabin to see her best friend strung over the wood stove. Robin pulled Paige off the stove, easing her to the floor. But it was too late. Paige's head lolled to the side, her tongue hanging out, her eyes wide open. Her neck had been broken. And she was no longer breathing.

"No!" Robin cried.

"It's not over!" a male voice said.

Robin glanced up to see the intruder standing at the open back door of the cabin.

It was Danny Kovack.

And he was going to kill Robin.

SEVENTEEN

Danny took a step toward Robin. She jumped to her feet, backing against the wall, grabbing a piece of firewood to use as a club. Danny hesitated, gazing at her with a strange expression.

"Don't come near me!" Robin cried.

Danny glanced down at Paige. "Oh no!" He stooped quickly, trying to help her.

"She's dead!" Robin screamed. "And you killed her."

Danny straightened his body, glaring at her. "No way, Robin. I didn't kill her. I just got here too late to save her!"

"Save her? You followed us up here to kill us! You're obsessed, Danny. You need help."

"Robin, it's not me! I swear!"

He took another step.

Robin raised the log to hit him. "Stay back!"

"You don't understand, Robin—"

"I understand everything, Danny. You followed us up here to kill us. You got to Paige first. Now you're after me!"

Danny shook his head. "No, you've got it all wrong. I didn't kill Paige! It was the guy on the snowmobile. I was watching the cabin. It took me all day to find this place. I had to sleep in my car last night, Robin. I came up here to protect you!"

"Protect me from what?" Robin challenged. "You're the one who lost it, Danny. You trashed the country club—"

"I figured out what happened, Robin. If you'll listen to me, I know why I acted like that at the country club. But it's not what you think. I love you, Robin."

She brandished the log, threatening to brain Danny if he came any closer to her. "You have a funny way of showing your love, Danny. Or is that how you treat Doreen? Does she like to be hurt? Do you act like a savage in front of her?"

"Robin, I'm not here to hurt you. The guy on the snowmobile did this. Can't you see—"

"If you don't want to hurt me, let me go," Robin told him.

Danny hesitated, grimacing. "But I'm not holding you hostage, I want to get you out of here, Robin. I want to take you home. We have to call the police because of Paige."

Robin's chest heaved as her lungs drew in cold air. She couldn't trust Danny, not with Paige lying dead on the floor. She had to get out of there, run to the car, drive to the nearest pay phone and call the police.

"If you don't want to hurt me, then let me go," Robin challenged again. "Let me walk out of here."

Danny smiled and gestured to her feet. "Robin, you aren't even wearing your shoes."

She glanced down for a moment at her stockinged feet.

"You can't walk out with no shoes on," Danny went on. "Here, take these."

He picked up a pair of boots.

Robin shivered. "Those were Paige's."

Danny unleashed a shudder in his body, quickly dropping the boots that had belonged to the dead girl. "Which ones are yours?" he asked. "Those maybe." He pointed to a pair of brown boots next to the wall.

Robin nodded, watching him, not sure what to expect. Was this a trick? Did he plan to catch her off guard and break *her* neck?

Danny threw the brown boots at her. "Go ahead, put them on. Go on, do it."

Robin glanced at the boots on the floor. "What's the catch, Danny?"

He shook his head. "No catch. Just put them on and we'll drive out of here."

Robin held the piece of wood in front of her.

"Put that down," Danny said. "I won't hurt you."

"Danny, why should I trust you?"

He put his hands on his hips, gazing at her with an impatient expression on his rugged face. "Look, princess, I could've already taken you out if I wanted to. That little chunk of firewood isn't going to do you any good against me."

"Oh, yeah?"

"Yeah!" Danny cried.

He lunged suddenly at her. Robin tried to hit him with the piece of wood. But Danny was too quick. He snatched the firewood from her so fast that Robin lost her balance and went tumbling to the floor. Danny stood over her, holding the log. Would he use it to smash her head?

Robin closed her eyes, drawing her legs into her chest, scrunching into a ball. "Don't kill me."

Danny lifted the log in front of him. "Don't be ridiculous. I'm not going to hurt you." He threw the wood toward the stove. It landed with a loud crash, prompting Robin to open her eyes.

"You didn't kill me!" she cried.

"Just put on the boots." Danny turned

away from her, gazing out the window. "Hurry. It's going to be dark soon. I want to get out of here before he comes back."

Robin grabbed her boots and started to pull them onto her cold feet. "Who are you talking about?"

He glanced back in her direction. "The same guy who made me go wacko at the dance. The guy who probably killed Candy."

"But Candy committed suicide!"

Danny shook his head. "No, she didn't. And I know who killed her and why he did it."

Robin tied the lace on her right boot. Danny had lost it. He was fantasizing, lost in his own world. He didn't seem crazy, but Robin knew that he was.

"Somebody slipped me angel dust at the country club," Danny went on, turning back to the window.

She pulled on the left boot and laced it tight.

"Somebody was after me, Robin."

His back was to her now!

"Robin, you have to believe me. I can explain it all if you'd just listen—"

She leapt to her feet, charging for the open front door.

Danny spun around to watch her go. "Robin, wait—"

But she wasn't taking any chances. She bolted for the Escort, which sat in the dirt driveway. Jumping into her car, she reached for the steering column. The keys weren't there! She'd have to flee on foot.

But as she was opening the door, Danny stepped up next to the Escort. He grabbed the top of the door before she could close it. Something dangled from his hand, clinking metal.

"You'll need these," he said.

He threw a key ring into the car and then let go of the door.

Danny held out his hands. "Go on. Leave! Get away from me! I don't care. I can hold my own against the guy on the snowmobile."

Robin gaped at him. "You're letting me go?"

"Get the police, bring them back here," Danny challenged. "I'll wait for you."

Robin picked up the keys, jamming the right one into the ignition switch. She turned the key but the car did not respond. The engine wouldn't turn over. Robin glared at Danny.

He frowned. "What?"

"You did this to the car!" she accused.

He sighed and shook his head. "No. Pop the hood, I'll take a look."

Robin hesitated. Did he really want to help her? Danny scowled and motioned for her to pull the hood release lever. When Robin complied, Danny looked under the hood but then quickly dropped it. He shook his head, grimacing.

"What?" Robin asked.

"He stole your plug wires. We'll have to walk out of here."

Robin got out of the car, pointing a finger at him. "Danny, tell me what's going on here."

"Robin, I told you, I'm innocent. If you'll just listen to me, I'll—uh oh, what's that?"

They both turned toward the whining sound that reverberated through the forest above the cabin. A pair of round lights cut between the trees. The snowmobile had returned.

Danny grabbed Robin's arm. "We've got to get out of here."

She stared at the lights. "Who—"

"It doesn't matter now, let's go."

Danny broke into a run, dragging Robin with him as he tried to flee down the dirt road. But the snowmobile circled around them, coming out on the trail ahead, forcing Danny to turn toward the lake. He ran again, taking Robin along.

Who were they running from? Robin wondered. Why was the snowmobile chasing them? Could Danny really be innocent?

They made it to the edge of the lake before the snowmobile came after them. The engine whined as the vehicle slid back onto the snow. He was coming slow, torturing them.

Danny glanced from side to side. The sky was growing darker. And the guy with the headlights had the advantage.

"What are we going to do?" Danny said to the wind.

Robin gazed out at the lake. "I think I know."

Danny glanced at her, his eyes wide. "Say it, princess."

"Follow me."

Robin darted onto the ice.

"Wait!" Danny cried

The snowmobile came out of the woods, driving straight toward Danny. Danny went after Robin, sliding on the ice, falling down. Robin scurried back to help him to his feet. They moved away from the snowmobile, heading for the middle of the lake.

"This is nuts," Danny said. "He'll catch us easy."

Robin gazed back at the menacing vehicle. The lights were sinister, glowing like the eyes of evil in the first purple shadows of dusk. Why was he just sitting there? Was he going to leave them alone? Or would they suffer the same fate as Paige?

"Who is he?" Robin asked.

"I'll tell you if you want to listen," Danny replied.

"Just keep moving. Hurry."

The ice was slippery. They were stumbling

more than running. And the snowmobile left
the shore finally, following Robin and Danny
onto the ice.

"He's coming," Danny muttered.

"Let him," Robin replied.

They slid over the frozen surface, trying to
maintain their balance. Danny slipped several times and went sprawling on his backside. Robin helped him to his feet, pulling
him farther and farther onto the ice.

The snowmobile circled them, going round
and round, tightening the ring with each
pass.

Danny grabbed his side, which was aching.
"I hope he doesn't have a gun," he muttered.

"Hurry," Robin urged, "I don't think we've
come far enough. We have to—damn him!"

The winter rec-vehicle shot past them, almost running over Danny and Robin.

Danny tried to stop. "It's no use, Robin. We
can't get away from him. It's like in the
history book—stand up and fight."

"No, move your ass, Kovack. Now!"

"You sound like my gym teacher," Danny
replied.

They kept sliding forward on the ice. The
snowmobile tightened the circle until it drew
alongside them. Danny finally skittered to a
halt. Robin hung on to Danny, staying with
him as the vehicle stopped too.

The snowmobile driver's face was hidden

behind the tinted face shield of the helmet. It had grown dark around them. But not too dark for Danny to see the weapon the driver pulled from a leather jacket.

"He's got a gun," Danny moaned. "I knew it."

Robin glared at their tormentor. "What a chicken you are! Hiding behind that mask. You're a jerk, Skip!"

Danny looked at her. "You figured it out."

"Take off the helmet, Skip," Robin said. "Or don't you have the guts to let us see your face before you kill us?"

One hand held a large pistol that was pointed at Robin and Danny. The other hand lifted the tinted visor. Skip Chesterton glared out at them, his face framed by the helmet.

"How'd you figure it out, Robin?" Skip asked.

A shudder ran through her body. It was really Skip. Everything that Danny had said was true.

"I told her most of it, Chesterton," Danny rejoined. "How you slipped that drug into my punch at the dance."

Skip shrugged. "I had to make you act like an ape, so Robin would come back to me, Kovack. You cooperated great."

"Yes, but I didn't cooperate," Robin replied. "I wouldn't come back to you, Skip. So you made threatening phone calls, you put that stupid drawing in my locker."

Skip sighed. "I really cared about you, Robin. But you blew me off for this Pitney punk."

Robin started to say something, but she hesitated. The weird sound had reached her ears. Skip couldn't hear it with the helmet on. She had to keep him talking.

"Why did you kill Paige?" she asked.

Skip shook his head. "I'll admit that didn't go right. I was going to make it look like Kovack did it. You know, one last chance for you to comfort me."

"Like with Candy?" Robin challenged.

"He had to kill Candy," Danny chimed in. "She knew he put that angel dust in my drink. She went along with Skip until she realized that everything he was doing was only so he could get you back, Robin."

Robin glanced down quickly. It was happening. She could hear it. But would it happen before it was too late?

Skip gestured with the gun. "You know, Kovack, you're pretty smart for a Pitney puke. And you won't believe how easy it was for me to make Candy look like she offed herself. I had a little fun before I killed her too."

Danny laughed in the face of their executioner. "I'd tell you to go to hell, Chesterton.

But I think you know the way on your own."

Skip lifted the pistol, aiming it at Danny. "Cute, Kovack. Let's make those your last words."

Robin felt the trembling beneath her feet. "No, Skip, wait."

Skip shook his head. "So long, Kovack."

Danny looked down too. "Hey, what—"

"You'll never get away with it, Skip!" Robin cried.

She had to stall for time. Danny knew what was happening. Just a few more seconds.

Skip's finger tightened on the trigger. "It'll be easy. Danny killed you and Paige, and then turned the gun on himself. Great headlines. You're gonna be in the paper, Kovack."

But Danny glanced at Robin. "What the—"

A loud cracking resounded in the night air. Suddenly the ice gave way beneath Skip and the heavy vehicle. "Huh?" was Skip's only reaction as the snowmobile sank beneath the surface of the lake, disappearing into the deep, dark water. Skip Chesterton went with the snow-craft, doomed by the safety belt around his waist. He had followed them to the thin ice where Robin had almost fallen through earlier that day.

Danny couldn't believe his eyes. "Skip? He just—whoa—"

Robin jumped back as Danny fell through the ice. His head bobbed up and down as he tried to swim. He wouldn't last long in the cold water.

Robin fell on her stomach, squirming to remove her heavy down jacket. "Hang on, Danny. Please."

She tossed the jacket toward him, holding one of the sleeves. Danny groped until he finally caught hold of the other sleeve. Robin pulled hard, but the ice in front of her kept cracking. She had to inch backward, pulling Danny with her.

"It's cold," he cried. "Robin, help me."

"I'm trying, Danny, I'm trying!"

The ice began to hold. Robin pulled harder, bringing Danny to the edge of the hole. She grabbed the back of his jacket, dragging him onto the ice. For a moment the cracking sound filled the night air. Robin stiffened, clinging to Danny. But they didn't fall into the lake. It was only the broken ice shifting in the hole.

Robin dragged Danny onto the thicker surface. "Can you stand up?" she asked.

He was shivering too violently to answer.

Robin had to drag him all the way back to the cabin. She closed the doors and stoked the stove. She wrapped Danny's trembling body in blankets and then heated water for hot cocoa.

"Robin—" Danny said it through chattering teeth. "Paige—"

Robin glanced down at the body. She removed a sheet from one of the bunks and draped it over Paige. Robin was numb inside, devoid of any feeling.

She made hot cocoa for herself and Danny. But she couldn't drink it.

Finally, she looked at Danny and told him that she had better walk up to the main road and flag down a car.

Danny nodded, agreeing with her.

Somebody had to tell the police that Skip Chesterton was now on the bottom of Thunder Lake.

EPILOGUE

The fifteenth of May was bright with spring sunshine. Robin Anderson strode down the hallway of the senior classroom building, heading toward her locker. When she reached the wall of lockers, she stopped to turn the dial of the combination lock. As soon as the door was open, a white envelope fluttered to the ground.

Robin picked up the envelope that bore her name in printed block letters. She opened the note from Danny. A smile broke over her lovely face and she tossed her blond hair.

Are we going to the prom or what? the message read.

Robin looked up to see Danny standing at the end of the corridor, watching her. She closed the locker and walked toward him. Danny grinned and met her halfway.

"Hi," Robin said. "I got your note."

Danny touched her shoulder for a moment. "So, are we going to the prom?"

Robin sighed and shrugged. "I don't know, Danny. Somehow, it just doesn't seem that important."

She thought of Candy and Paige. Neither one of them had deserved to die. It had taken a while to convince the authorities that Skip had been responsible for their deaths and for putting the drug in Danny's punch at the country club dance.

But everything had been resolved, except for the sense of grief felt by her and Danny. Getting back together with Danny had helped Robin, even though her parents had not approved. Still, they let her spend time with Danny and she had been tutoring him again. Danny was going to graduate with a solid B average. And he had secured a student loan to go on to Port City Community College.

The future looked brighter, though the dreams and nightmares kept coming night after night. Danny had nightmares too. There was no way to completely escape the bad memories, though they grew a little dimmer each day.

"I always wanted to go to the prom with a classy girl like you," Danny offered. "I mean,

you aren't afraid that I'll go ballistic again if
I put on a tux, are you?"

"Danny! Don't be ridiculous."

Several of the faculty advisers had asked
Robin to be on the prom committee. But she
had declined. Robin had also given up the
soccer team. None of it seemed relevant to
her life, not with Candy and Paige lying in
Old Cemetery.

Danny gazed into her eyes. "You're thinking about Paige, aren't you?"

She nodded. "Are you still having the
dreams?"

"I wish I weren't," Danny replied. "Come
on, I'll walk you to your car."

Robin fell in beside him, striding toward
the end of the corridor. Danny had been so
sweet. She cared about him. If she stayed in
Port City to go to the community college after
graduation, their relationship might become
serious. It was sort of confusing, though she
had come to rely on Danny's support of late.
He hadn't pressured her about anything.
Instead, he had been her friend—her best
friend, in fact.

They left the building, emerging in the
warm air of the spring day. Danny took her
hand as they started for the senior parking
lot. Some of the student body members
shunned Robin because of her relationship

with Danny, but she didn't care. They didn't know Danny, not the way she knew him.

"You know something?" Danny said suddenly. "I'm glad Skip got what was coming to him."

"Danny!"

"No, I mean it. He was a jerk. And we didn't really kill him. Did we?"

"Well, no—"

"So he got what he deserved. He brought it all on himself. He killed Paige and Candy. Not us. We're innocent, Robin. We were the victims. There's no other way to look at it."

Robin stopped by her car, leaning against the Escort. "Danny, I guess you're right."

"I know I am," he replied. "If we feel sorry for anyone, it should be Paige and Candy. We shouldn't feel sorry for Skip. He was a freakin' psycho."

"I know."

Tears formed in her eyes.

Danny sighed. "We shouldn't feel sorry for ourselves either, Robin. At least we're alive."

She wiped the tears away, nodding.

Danny gazed into her blue irises. "So, are we on for the prom? It would mean a lot to me."

Robin laughed a little. "Why?"

"So I can show everyone I'm not a jerk," Danny replied. "That I can act nice in public."

"Oh, all right. I'll go."

"Thanks. I appreciate it."

Robin tilted her face toward the sky. Danny lowered his mouth. Their lips met in a brief kiss. Then he embraced Robin, holding her tightly, wishing that she would never let go.

"It's going to be okay," he told her.

Robin buried her face in his chest, thinking that this time he might be right.

Nicholas Pine

TERROR ACADEMY: STUDENT BODY

Abbey Wilder is a bright and popular senior, a cheerleader and straight-A student. And the victim of an attacker who clearly intended to kill her!

While the police search desperately for clues, Abbey's memory of the attack fades completely. But not the strange visions that seem to be warning her: this killer has rampaged before – and is about to strike again . . .

A Selected List of Fiction from Mammoth

While every effort is made to keep prices low, it is sometimes necessary to increase prices at short notice. Mandarin Paperbacks reserves the right to show new retail prices on covers which may differ from those previously advertised in the text or elsewhere.

The prices shown below were correct at the time of going to press.

☐	7497 1409 3	**Not Just Dancing**	Helen Flint	£2.99
☐	7497 1073 X	**Dying to Win**	Eileen Goudge	£2.99
☐	7497 0487 X	**Wait Till Helen Comes**	Mary Downing Hahn	£2.99
☐	7497 1460 3	**The Dead Hour**	Pete Johnson	£3.50
☐	7497 0281 8	**The Homeward Bounders**	Diana Wynne Jones	£3.50
☐	7497 1265 1	**Mandragora**	David McRobbie	£3.50
☐	7497 1061 6	**A Little Love Song**	Michelle Magorian	£3.99
☐	7497 1482 4	**Writing in Martian**	Andrew Matthews	£2.99
☐	7497 0323 7	**Silver**	Norma Fox Mazer	£3.50
☐	7497 0325 3	**The Girl of his Dreams**	Harry Mazer	£2.99
☐	7497 0280 X	**Beyond the Labyrinth**	Gillian Rubinstein	£2.50
☐	7497 0558 2	**Frankie's Story**	Catherine Sefton	£2.99
☐	7497 1291 0	**The Spirit House**	William Sleator	£2.99
☐	7497 0764 X	**Pebble on the Beach**	Ian Strachan	£2.99
☐	7497 0009 2	**Secret Diary of Adrian Mole**	Sue Townsend	£3.50
☐	7497 1015 2	**Come Lucky April**	Jean Ure	£2.99
☐	7497 0147 1	**A Walk on the Wild Side**	Robert Westall	£3.50

All these books are available at your bookshop or newsagent, or can be ordered direct from the address below. Just tick the titles you want and fill in the form below.

Cash Sales Department. PO Box 5. Rushden, Northants NN10 6YX.
Fax: 0933 410321 . Phone 0933 410511.

Please send cheque, payable to 'Reed Book Services Ltd.', or postal order for purchase price quoted and allow the following for postage and packing:

£1.00 for the first book. 50p for the second: **FREE POSTAGE AND PACKING FOR THREE BOOKS OR MORE PER ORDER.**

NAME (Block letters) ....

ADDRESS ....

....

☐ I enclose my remittance for ....

☐ I wish to pay by Access/Visa Card Number

Expiry Date

Signature ....

Please quote our reference: MAND